SECRET KILLS

Also by William Beechcroft

Position of Ultimate Trust
Image of Evil
Chain of Vengeance
The Rebuilt Man

SECRET KILLS

William Beechcroft

DODD, MEAD & COMPANY
NEW YORK

"There are all sorts of things that I suppose could be done. There are many things that need to be done secretly, and we have to have a greater capacity in our country to recognize the importance of being able to do things without having them publicized ahead of time."

Secretary of State George Shultz,
interviewed on the CBS program,
Face the Nation, April 1986.

This is a work of fiction. All characters and incidents are products of the author's imagination.

Published by Dodd, Mead & Company, Inc.
71 Fifth Avenue, New York, New York 10003
Manufactured in the United States of America
First Edition

1 2 3 4 5 6 7 8 9 10

Library of Congress Cataloging-in-Publication Data

Beechcroft, William.
    Secret kills/William Beechcroft.—1st ed.
        p.   cm.
    I. Title.
PS3552.E32S4   1988
813'.54—dc19   87-34042
ISBN 0-396-09062-1

1

MYRA STANFIELD hated Penn Station, but she liked the Metroliner to Washington a lot better than Eastern's aerial shuttle. Penn Station, though perpetually jammed, tainted with diesel fumes and nervous sweat smell, its concourse stairways havens for unsavory street people, its restrooms unthinkable, was an easy taxi ride from Columbia's brick walkways. And the Metroliner did not activate her palm-dampening doubt of the ability of a soaring jet to pick its way safely through Long Island's cluttered airborne traffic.

At twenty, Myra had discovered that life was a back-to-back series of compromises. She had hoped to go to Harvard, but the best acceptance had come from Columbia. She had expected—and had been expected—to follow her father's lead into law, but the major she was now more certain she could manage was journalism. She had hoped that Brett would invite her to his parents' Connecticut place for Christmas, but the relationship had downgraded from savor to simmer to sulk, so now she was headed for the holidays with Father.

Not that the visit would be uninteresting. Under Secretary of State Edwin Stanfield would do his best as both father and surrogate mother to provide eligibles. There would be the inevitable cocktail party at the quite grand, if rented, Stanfield residence in Fairfax. The elegantly maintained stable with its two Morgan mares would be handily available. And Washington, of course, was a city infinitely more exciting than her native Baltimore. There just would be no Brett Tilton, no languorous Sunday mornings in bed, both of them wonderfully naked and drowsily hungry for each other.

Compromise.

The Checker rattled off Thirty-third into the funneled passage between Madison Square Garden and Penn Station's main entrance. She paid the dark foreign-looking driver and shoved her suitcase out ahead of her. The mid-morning December air smelled of exhaust, charcoal smoke from a chestnut vendor upwind on Thirty-third, and that underlying Manhattan savor she had once described to Brett as "restoration soot."

The down escalator to the main floor was jammed with Christmas departees. She was conveyor-belted into a swirl of people, each isolated in concern for his or her own purpose there. The effect was a perpetual and intense headlong scurry.

She picked through the crowd in the shopping arcade, was mightily jostled by a heedless woman in a hideous orange monkey fur jacket in front of the Hoffritz window, then emerged into the echoing, high-ceilinged concourse. Her dark hair already needed a comb. Her pixie face was flushed with a combination of resentment at the crowd's impatient self-concern and the sudden realization that she was running late.

She forced herself to stop to read the big Arrival/ Departure board suspended over the grouped wooden

2

benches. The Washington-bound Metroliner was scheduled out of East Gate 10 in just four minutes!

Gate 10 was diagonally across the jammed floor. She took a tighter grip on her suitcase and plunged through the crowd. A large man in a fur-collared overcoat stepped smack in front of her. Of all the—

Across the concourse, the last stragglers of the cluster around the departure gate were funneling through the narrow entrance to the escalator that would carry them to the track below. She dodged around the slow-moving man.

—And the whole place dissolved in a flash of brilliant yellow light. A wave of heat slapped her face and hands. A clap of hard sound struck her as if she had run full tilt into an invisible barrier.

She felt her suitcase tear from her paralyzed fingers. Skewers of pain thrust through her ears straight into her brain. She heard a woman scream—a howl of agony and terror that faded into echoing distance. Then she heard nothing.

At that moment in the shabby offices of the national biweekly tabloid *NewsLeak,* not far north on Seventh Avenue, Dan Forrest was grinding out the final paragraph of a follow-up story on a certain Jacob Ashkanazi, a just-nabbed alleged killer of South Bronx street people. He had the misleading habit of delivering a lecture on work habits to his victims before he delivered the fatal knife thrust—or so the latest victim had claimed in the paramedic van just before he made the siren unnecessary.

This intriguing eyewitness report enabled Dan to tag Ashkanazi "Jake the Rapper," a fortuitous tag that had upped the New York metro sales of the tabloid's most recent edition by nine percent.

3

When the Penn Station concourse blew, Dan could not have had the remotest inkling that the grisly incident was about to have a far greater impact on him than his currently high-flying Rapper series ever would. Nor could he have in any way foreseen that a seemingly unrelated death, two weeks hence, would become part of a story that would relegate Ashkanazi to page 23. In fact, Dan might not have become involved at all, were it not for his Cousin Roy. Leroy Forrest, Detective 2nd Grade, NYPD.

4

2

DETECTIVE LEROY FORREST was ready for a corpse this chilly January morning. But he wasn't ready for the one he found on the fourteenth floor of the Chelsea Carlisle—actually the thirteenth, but even in this enlightened age, designated 14.

In the elevator, he mulled what Kilcullen had blurted down in the lobby when Roy Forrest had come in from freeze-dried Seventy-seventh, pulled off his gloves and blown on his fingers. Kilcullen, one of the two uniforms from the RMP unit angled to the curb outside, had detailed himself to wait in the lobby for Roy, once he and Silvestro, his partner, had gotten a look at what was in 1407. The swarthy cop didn't look shocked, as he might have at a particularly grisly find up there. But he didn't look complacent, either. Mystified, maybe?

Forrest wasn't the swiftest gold shield in the squad, but that much he could read in Kilcullen's eyes and in the odd way he shook his head when Roy questioned him.

"Not a wet one?" Roy deduced.

"No, it ain't that. It's who it is, and how it was done to her."

Roy Forrest rode the elevator alone, which was something of a surprise considering who the stiff was. But these were the early moments of what was certain to be a big one. The city that never sleeps was only half awake this time of day. And contrary to popular versions, the investigations of most unnatural deaths—even the notable ones—began with the appearance of a couple of patrol cops. Then, if luck held, next on the scene was the precinct detective who was catching when their call was logged in. The stampede of forensic people and, inevitably, the media buzzards, came later, including more often than not *NewsLeak* in the person of Roy's cousin, Dan Forrest. So far this morning, though, luck had held. The death of a national celebrity was, as yet, unexploited.

The walnut-paneled elevator whispered to its fourteenth floor halt. Its door slid open on a hallway carpeted in plush cream and blue. Grasscloth, Roy thought they called it, textured the walls. Bronze lighting fixtures. Mellow.

Fourteen-oh-seven wasn't hard to find because Kilcullen's partner stood in front of it, hands clasped behind his oversized butt in parade rest. He was a bigger cop than Kilcullen, with a wedge of blue jaw.

When he swung his head Roy's way, his thick brows jerked up. They already knew each other from the gory aftermath of the Penn Station blast a little over two weeks back. All right, you bastard, Roy thought, go ahead and wonder why they sent Kong the Plodder out on this one. Damned if I'll tell him I was the only gold shield free when the call came.

Roy nodded. "Morning, Silvestro. Not much of a crowd."

6

"Not in this place, Forrest. People mind their business in this place."

"Or they don't get up this early. Who found her?"

"Maid."

"This time of day?"

"Not like a hotel maid. Her personal maid. More of a housekeeper. She has a key. Comes in six days a week to straighten up the kitchen, make breakfast before she cleans." Silvestro had an asthmatic wheeze.

"Week in, week out?"

"Whenever Falconer was here."

"Where is she?"

Silvestro gave him an odd look. "Hell, she's in there, Forrest."

"I mean the maid. I'll want to talk to her."

"Oh. She's pretty well unglued. There's a house doctor has an apartment and office down on three. I woke him up and had Kilcullen take her down to him."

"You didn't leave once you got up here?"

Silvestro shot him a disdainful look. "And I didn't touch nothing, either."

Forrest let the sarcasm roll by. He was used to it. He *was* a plodder. They were right about that. He knew he lacked the quick intuition expected of a homicide cop by everyone except the gold shields themselves. Every man on the squad knew that persistence paid off a hell of a lot more often than flash and dash.

"Okay," he said to Silvestro. "Let's go on in."

The big cop turned the brass knob that was fashionably but awkwardly centered in the paneled door, and they stepped inside. If Roy had gone no farther than the foyer, he would have been impressed. The floor was parquet, still tight and lustrous after fifteen years of Chelsea Carlisle rentals. The walls were flocked green with gold pinstriping. A chandelier here? Brass and crystal, small but elegant. The big mirror over the antique hall table was framed in gold leaf.

"No pain," Silvestro said into the silence.

The living room was down two carpeted steps into space, lots of beige space, with low blond Swedish modern to add to the impression. The immense picture window across the wall-to-wall's acreage was blanketed by heavy eggshell drapes. The place reeked of lavish overspending, but not yet of death.

"Dining room and kitchen's through there." Silvestro angled a thumb leftwards. "Bedrooms on the other side."

They crushed across the spongy carpeting, entered a hallway papered with exotic birds among bamboo.

"Three bedrooms?"

"Doorman told us she had friends here off and on. Most the time she was here alone. Only used the place, though, when she was in a play or here to promote a movie."

Roy nodded, then looked at Silvestro expectantly.

"She's in the big one. At the end of the hall."

Silvestro was not quite accurate about that. The body wasn't in the over-frilled salmon and white bedroom. It was in the bathroom.

"Jeez . . ." Roy breathed.

Marguerite Falconer had been a beautiful woman, blessed with the delicate features that movie and TV cameras, even with their electronic ten pounds added, flattered. She wasn't beautiful now.

Roy stood in the bathroom doorway, his heart thudding in the claustrophobic silence. Behind him, he heard Silvestro's asthmatic breathing. Roy thought she would be bigger than the huddled corpse in the empty tub, but that, obviously, had been an illusion of the big screen.

Maybe the leading men they'd given her had been small guys.

"What do you think?" Roy said. "Maybe five-three or four?"

"Hard to say, her all doubled up like that."

"Like that" was like nothing Roy had come across in his twelve years on the job. Four of them as a gold shield. The actress was jackknifed on her knees. She had sagged against the far side of the pink porcelain. Her head had fallen forward. Her smooth, shoulder-length cornsilk hair obscured the lower part of her face, but the familiar upturned nose and now grotesquely bulging amber eyes were unmistakably Marguerite Falconer's.

There was no water in the tub, but she was naked. Roy had seen his share of nude corpses, raped and beaten purple, razor-slashed crimson, cold gray from overdose, bluishly holed by .32s and .38s. Nonentities all, except for their brief postmortem filings in the *New York Post* and *Daily News*—or maybe in Cousin Dan Forrest's national rag, if there was more to it than a street kill. But the kneeling corpse of Marguerite Falconer, star of *Giants from Acorns Grow*—an Oscar winner, for God's sake—struck Roy as the most flagrantly obscene assignment he'd had wished on him to date.

" . . . to date!" he muttered.

"What?" Silvestro wheezed behind him.

"You and Kilcullen found her just like this?"

"Damn it, I told you—"

"Okay, okay. Sorry."

Roy was struck by the smallness of her breasts. Like a young girl's. Falconer was what? Close to forty? Settling blood had colored the lower part of her body. She'd been like this long enough for that to take place.

9

The body's crouch was unusual, but not unique. What got Roy to wondering how in hell he would write up his DD5 was the rest of it.

Her arms were handcuffed behind her. The interlaced fingers grasped the end of a heavy cord, a woven length of some shiny gold stuff. "Silk, maybe?" he asked Silvestro absently. It was a quarter-inch thick and long enough to loop from her hands up over the shower curtain rod, then back down to Marguerite Falconer's neck. The cord was wrapped around the slender throat, not in a noose, but in a double coil that had apparently been secured by tension on the cord.

Even that bizarre arrangement wasn't what riveted Roy's eyes, in spite of his uncomfortable feeling that he was invading a public figure's final privacy. He stared at the markings. A heavy ring of apple-red lipstick had been drawn around the areola of her right breast. Roy crouched. "Yeah, on both of them."

Crowding forty, she was still so slender that, even crouched forward, her compressed abdomen failed to obscure the crude lipstick sunrise that arched above the tan pubic tuft at the juncture of the clamped thighs.

Silvestro rasped uncomfortably close to Roy's ear, "What the hell does *that* say?" They both bent down.

The vivid lipstick lettering below her breasts was partially hidden by her elbows.

"E . . . L . . . E . . . A, and under that, it looks like an A, a P, then T, and a U. Rest of it's hidden by her arms." Roy stood and fingered his chin. "Cuff key and lipstick tube right here on the tub ledge. What the hell is this?" He glanced around. "This place as neat as this when you—"

"Damn, Forrest! How many times do I have to tell you?"

10

"Sorry. It just don't fit a homicide. Not a sign of a struggle. Whole place is like *House Beautiful* is coming to do a feature. Well, time to call forensics. Not on that phone out there. Use your hand unit to Kilcullen."

Silvestro couldn't raise Kilcullen from the apartment. He went out in the hall. With the blunt end of a ballpoint, Roy flipped open the medicine cabinet. Hand creams, face creams, skin lotion, one of those toothpaste pumps, three toothbrushes. How about that? Three. Tylenol. No prescriptions? He'd thought Hollywood types were heavy into that. Circular box of birth control pills, the first seven of them gone. Divorced, wasn't she? Couple of years ago.

He shut the cabinet door and looked down at the pathetic little body. Not a drop of blood, he thought, but it's got me shook anyway. Because it's her, and because of the way it's been done. Who but a nut would take somebody out like this?

Twenty-seven minutes later, the apartment was crawling with technician types, and Roy's presence had become secondary. "I'll need the lab report as soon as I can get it," he told the medical examiner.

"Boy, oh boy," said that fascinated white-haired gnome of death. He stood with his hands on his skinny hips, gazing into the dry tub with bright bird eyes. "Boy, oh boy!"

To his surprise, Roy had his hands on the report a little after four. Slow day at Bellevue? He scanned it. Then he sat down abruptly and read it slowly.

"I'll be damned!" he exploded in the near-empty squad room. Across the aisle, Detective Ed Farnay's close-set watery eyes looked up briefly. Kong was given to occasional outbursts like this, as if the job was sometimes a jump ahead of him.

Roy stared at the ME's verdict.

11

"Accident?" he blurted. *"Accident!"* By God, it looked like he actually needed Cousin Dan on this one.

By now, *NewsLeak* had carried Dan Forrest's Jake the Rapper follow-up and his "I was there" report on the Penn Station Massacre. He had been there, but a half hour after it had happened, not when it happened. But there were ways and ways to write a thing like that. Dan's instincts occasionally queazed at Charlie Lovett's way with Dan's words. But Charlie was the editor and *NewsLeak*'s stateside boss. So "I almost witnessed" became "Eyewitnessed." What was a half hour?

The Falconer thing, though, came to Dan's attention over the wires—a much quieter delivery mode than the screeching sirens on Seventh Avenue that had converged on smoke-choked Penn Station. At first, he mentally tagged the death of an actress to be a lesser story, maybe even more of a Corkie Brion story: a one-edition page-two blat, then to the bird cage bottoms. Nothing at this early date would have made him remotely suspect they were parts of the same story. Or that he was about to become one of its principal concerns. Certainly, he had no inkling that the Penn Station bombing and a movie star's death would lead to a contract to kill him.

3

ON THE EVENING of the day Marguerite Falconer was found huddled, graffitied, and dead in her bathroom, Dan Forrest—only an unwitting hour from involvement in the story that could cost him his life—dragged into his East Side brownstone apartment burdened with something more than standard depression. Standard depression he could live with. It came from the job and the subway commute. Nothing like the BMT's mobile laboratory of human anxiety to set the old nerves atwang.

And the job, a helluva comedown from the mountaintop, was far from therapeutic. The job, he blamed on himself. *The New York Times* had been at the top of the bottle. The *Daily News,* halfway down. The Long Island weekly, damned near the bottom, where a screaming nightmare at Bellevue lay in the dregs. *NewsLeak,* in fact, was partway up again—now that he was dry. Maybe it was as far up as he was going to get.

He couldn't kick about the pay. In far off Wales, absentee landlord Llewellan Markelhenny had a surprisingly generous people purse. *NewsLeak*'s salaries were almost inspiring, but that was where the Cardiff Giant drew the line. The tabloid's digs on Seventh were 1950s rehab, without a hint of state-of-the-art retrofit. The wire service clackers were only as new as necessary. The six plywood editorial cubicles had made it only to aged Selectrics, whose self-correcting progeny were a long way down the geneological line.

Bottoming out those persistent downers of the clearance sale office environment and the kamikaze commute thereto and therefrom was today's product of Dan's attempt to do a neighbor a favor. Casey Pickett, tenant of the apartment across the first floor hall, had been sent by her computer service company on a three-month tour of duty in Texas to help set up a new system for a Fort Worth client. "It's a promotion, Daniel, but a major pain in the butt. I don't even have time to find a subleaser. Do you think maybe you could turn up . . . uh, well, as a favor, maybe somebody you know?"

She had bestowed highly personal favors of her own from time to time, so he was morally stuck. His mistake had been to mention the matter to *NewsLeak*'s prime office broadcaster, Jonathan Blauvelt. Within twelve minutes, Blauvelt had pirouetted through Dan's cell door with, "I have a taker, dear man."

"A taker?"

"For the sublease, for heaven's sake."

"Who?" Dan's tone was wary, yet hopeful. For a nanosecond, his heart had hopped. Was it remotely possible that the breath-stopping Melody Matso—

"Not Melody," Blauvelt mind-read. "Corkie."

A half-formed vision of Melody's lush proximity went ashatter. Dan ran fingers through his thinning pale hair, absently scratched his slightly askew nose. And sighed. Cornelia Brion for a neighbor? The prospect had haunted the entire day thereafter. Then his depression

14

had been nadired by Corkie's nonignorable hundred-sixty-pound presence on the homeward subway, bouncing easily beside him through the several blocks thereafter, close behind on the brownstone's worn steps like a persistent St. Bernard.

She had just *loved* Casey's apartment. "Even the darling computer, printer, and modem, I think they call it, and all that other impressive electronic crap in the spare bedroom. What is she, Daniel, a KGB agent?"

"She's in the data systems business. That stuff's her homework."

"So I'll live around it. I'm sold."

My God, she was going to be across the hall for the next three months! Corkie Brion breathing, eating, and sleeping not fifty feet away. What had he done to merit such. . . . Hell, he was trapped already, here in the hall.

"How about a sandwich?" he offered in resignation.

They ate in silence; uneasy from his side of the enameled steel kitchen table, confidently serene from hers. She attacked his ham and cheese and pumpernickel with immodest enthusiasm. They'd gnawed through almost a quarter loaf, and she showed no signs of waning.

"So," he said into the looming silence, "how's the celebrity business?" Inane, but talking about the other guy's work was a sure conversational hit, and she was *NewsLeak*'s scandal reporter.

"The celeb business," she said from behind a third sandwich, "is always in season. Rutting season."

Oh, it was going to be that kind of talk?

"A is sleeping with B's husband, who was seen with C's wife, who's suing A."

God or somebody save me, Dan pleaded mutely.

Then . . . reprieve? The thuds on his apartment door were the signature of only one ham-handed author.

15

More inhibited people used the buzzer, but Cousin Roy enjoyed authoritative thunder.

He shouldered in and peered toward the clank of kitchen steelware. "You got Casey back there?"

"She done left me, Cousin. Florida for three months. I got her replacement back there."

Corkie abruptly blocked the kitchen access, licking her fingers. "Hi. Corkie Brion."

Roy stared, first at her, then at Dan.

"A colleague, Roy. She writes our who-stripped-Joan stuff. She's subleasing Casey's digs." He rolled his eyes ceilingward. Roy seemed to get it. Do somebody a favor and punishment is not far behind.

"You got a spare beer?"

"One of those days?" Roy was as predictable as moonrise. Tough case days often brought him here for an unwinding before he continued his homeward schlep to Barb out in the Long Island wilds.

With a Miller's, Roy sprawled across Dan's big sofa and gestured with the bottle. "She all right?"

"How would he know?" Corkie asked around the last of the sliced ham. "I just got here."

Roy scowled at Dan. "You know what I mean."

"Cousin Roy Forrest means he wants to talk," Dan informed Corkie from the hard side chair he was forced into when she unerringly took his lounger. "It's against department regs, and if we blab, Cousin Roy's nethers will be in a sling."

Corkie shrugged impressive shoulders beneath her layered drapes. "Mum as gum. What's this 'cousin' bit?"

"Brothers for fathers makes you cousins. So I have a cop cousin. You want to take her word, Roy, it's up to you."

"She blows this, and we're done, Cousin. You hear that?"

"You hear that?" Dan relayed.

"I hear it. He knows where we work, and he's willing to talk cases?"

"Sometimes it's therapy. And sometimes I'm a freer agent than he is, if you know what I mean."

Her substantial eyebrows rose over an intense brown stare. "Ah, so." She had finished the third sandwich. Now her chunky fingers locked around a knee. She gazed at Roy. "Lead on, MacDuff."

"It's lay on," Dan said.

"We barely know each other, but it's a thought."

Roy shot her a confused look, broke it for a drag on his bottle, belched softly against closed lips. "It's the Falconer thing."

"Yeah, we got it on the wires around noon."

"You only got what we told the vultures, Dan. Dead in her apartment this morning. Accident in the bathtub. Before the media guys got to us, the PC's office had a clamp on it. So that's all we could let them have. If you'd seen— You wouldn't believe it. Hell, she was a national figure. Anyway, the medical examiner's report says accident."

"Wait a minute!" Corkie blurted. "Are *you* on that case?"

"I was the detective assigned."

"Hot *damn!*"

"Corkie, you can't do it."

"Charlie's already given it to me, Daniel. You know he did that when it came over as an accident."

"I don't care what Charlie's done. This is a privileged conversation, and you can't use any part of it without Roy's say-so."

"You've got to be kidding!"

"I'm not kidding. Either you go along with that, or you get your purse and go along. Right now."

"You're not kidding. A tabloid reporter with a conscience?"

"No, one with a hell of an NYPD contact that I'm not about to jeopardize. Pardon the frankness, Roy."

"Cuts both ways."

"Well, hell," Corkie grumbled. "Okay, okay."

Roy gave her a long stare. "Damnedest accident I ever saw." He described the bizarre state in which he'd found Marguerite Falconer's naked body. "When the ME got her straightened out, the lipstick letters spelled RELEASE, and below that, RAPTURE."

"What kind of an accident is that?"

"Same thing I wondered, Cousin. Also wondered how she wrote so neat, and upside down for her, with the lipstick. Wondered about the whole scene, then down came word from the PC to close it up. Could be same word went to the ME. His report called it. . . . What the hell was it? 'Autoerotic asphyxia.' "

"Dekker!" Corkie burst out.

They looked at her blankly.

"Albert Dekker—1960s. They found him the same way—nude in his tub. Handcuffed, rope around his neck with the end of it in his hands. Words in lipstick."

"Words like hers?" Roy rumbled.

"Worse, plus an obscene sketch. He also had a hypo stuck in each arm, scarf over his eyes, some kind of weird horse's bit in his mouth, assorted thongs and belts."

"Jeez! What did they call *that*?"

"Suicide first, Roy. Then accidental death."

"I thought I was the crime reporter," Dan said.

"We're talking celebrities here, my dear. Noguchi—"

"The L.A. coroner?" Roy wasn't going to be outclassed.

"He called it what you said: autoerotic asphyxia."

18

"Which specifically is what?" Dan asked.

"I thought you were the crime reporter."

"I'm at home with a nice, understandable shooting or knife job, Cork, but autoerotic—People *hang* themselves for kicks?"

"The ME's report said it's common in kinky circles." Roy grimaced. "The idea seems to be to come right to the hairy edge of choking yourself. That's supposed to bring on—" He glanced at Corkie.

"An orgasm," she said.

"Uh, yeah. I can think of better ways." Roy studied the beer bottle. "Anyway, the handcuffs are almost always part of it. Ritual stuff, I guess."

"How about the lipstick scrawlings?"

"The report didn't say they were ritual, Dan, but after what Corkie just told us about that guy in L.A.—"

"Albert Dekker." She looked surprised that the name hadn't registered. "He was one fine actor, guys. More than a hundred movies, legit stage, even served in the California State Assembly, then the McCarthy thing got him. But he made a comeback. Don't tell me neither of you ever saw *The Wild Bunch* on the late show?"

"What was he doing with that bathtub, rope, and cuffs routine?"

"That's what a lot of people wondered, Roy. There was talk of missing money, a lot of it. And he'd always been considered straight, had been married, had kids, was engaged to marry again. But the police never reversed their 'accident' theory."

"So, here we are again? Only I don't believe it. Not Marguerite Falconer."

"You were a fan!"

Roy frowned at her. "Guess it shows."

Dan swirled the coffee dregs in his thick NY Mets mug. "Why don't you think it was accidental, Roy? Aside from who it was."

"That's my problem. Gut feeling, I guess. The ME reported no signs of sexual abuse. I didn't see any evidence of a struggle. The place was neat as a barrack on inspection day. I gave it a good going-over before the lab boys showed up. Nothing out of place that I could find. She wasn't on anything. No needle marks, no pills except Tylenol and birth control. That's the hell of it. The evidence supports the ME's report. I just can't see the likes of her going to all that trouble with handcuffs, a rope over the curtain rod, the lipstick artwork. Just doesn't seem in character."

"How do you know what her real character was?" Corkie shrugged. "She might have been kinky as Calvados in the privacy of her boudoir."

"If she got her kicks with a rope, why would she be on the pill?" Dan wondered.

"Sometimes just to regulate periods," Corkie said.

Roy scowled. "You're a regular encyclopedia."

"Well, he asked."

"Time of death, by the way, was between midnight and about two A.M.," Roy told them. "No earlier."

"If you think something's off-center, you can start by interviewing all known acquaintances, can't you?"

"No, Dan, I can't. That's the problem. I told you the case is closed. As of late this afternoon."

"Word came from the PC, you said? Why would the Police Commissioner himself put the clamps on?"

"I haven't the remotest, Cousin. But it don't sit right with me."

"Because it's Marguerite Falconer?"

20

"No, Dan, because it's the PC. You asked it yourself. Why would *he* send down word?" Roy shrugged. "Well, now you know why I'm here."

"I thought it was for the therapeutic value of a friendly ear. That's usually why."

Roy nodded. "Yeah, it's that. But it's more. I'm off the case. There is no case. I can't do another damned thing about it."

"But I can?"

Roy smiled for the first time since he'd clumped in. "You got it, Cousin Dan'l. Keep in touch, but make damned sure you keep me out of your typewriter."

A significant development took place fourteen hours later and two hundred and fifty miles south. The meet was in a sprawling motel complex just off Interstate-270 in Rockville, Maryland. The two men in business gray blended into the luncheon crowd. They could have been two bureaucrats from the nearby Department of Commerce annex or two execs from any of a dozen high-tech companies that had mushroomed along the interstate's industrial corridor.

They were neither of these, and neither was using his true name. "Mr. Johnson" was the larger of the two, a cultured-looking man with a high forehead over intense aquamarine eyes and a halo of white rimming his bald pate. The other man, known to Johnson as "Hammermill," was one of those compact men whose assertiveness more than made up for a five-foot-eight stature. His squared-off black mustache, stark ebony eyebrows, and oddly brush-cut, thick dark hair—surely he touched up the temples, Johnson decided—gave him an unsettling foreign appearance, though he had the unmistakable drawl of the Carolinas.

"Why in hell would anyone name a dining room after Billy Budd?" Johnson asked rhetorically from behind his oversized menu. "Wasn't he hanged for treason?"

"I wouldn't know." Hammermill's voice was flat, without interest. "I'll have the minute steak, broiled, not fried," he told the waitress.

"French fries or baked?"

"Baked, no butter, no sour cream. Fried stuff can kill you," he informed Johnson.

"The salmon. Tossed salad, house dressing." Johnson flipped the menu closed and handed it to the overweight brunette as she plodded away. "I doubt you'll live long enough in your profession, Hammermill, to worry about the deleterious effect of French fries."

"Part of my business is to keep fit. The other part is to do what I'm paid to do."

"I note that the initial action, according to this morning's *Post,* has been accomplished satisfactorily."

"That's why we're here."

"They called it 'accidental death.' I'd say that fulfills just a part of the requirement."

"Part?"

"You'll recall that the bizarre circumstances of Marguerite Falconer's death were intended as a diversion, something to keep the media on a compelling but securely isolated sidetrack."

"The field tactics were accomplished as planned, Johnson. The strategy is your end. If you want my opinion, I'd say somebody, somebody more than medium high, has put a muzzle on the NYPD. But that's not my problem. It's yours. You want the thing overt, you pull your own strings."

Johnson held Hammermill's unsettling gaze for less than five seconds. Then he looked down at the tablecloth.

22

The man radiated purpose with a gun muzzle's conscience.

"You are quite correct. Elimination under diverting circumstances was the requirement. I agree, that was accomplished." Johnson reached into his breast pocket and, with a crooked little smile, openly handed Hammermill a small box wrapped in white tissue and tied with a blue ribbon.

"What the hell is this?"

Johnson lowered his voice to a murmur. "The balance of payment for services to date—five thousand-dollar bills."

"Gift wrapped?"

"You have any idea what kind of excitement a plain white envelope raises in the State of Maryland?"

"You could have given me this in the parking lot."

"We could have met in Rock Creek Park or at the Lincoln Memorial or in my apartment. I just happen to think restaurants are less conspicuous. I wonder if you are more paranoid than I?"

"Because one is paranoid, they say, does not mean he is not justified in being that way."

"Your mastery of double negatives could qualify you for at least a GS-12 slot."

"Freelance pays better." Hammermill touched the new bulge in his suitcoat pocket. "Now, I presume, we can move on to the main course?"

Johnson looked up from fidgeting fingers, expecting to see the waitress approaching with their lunches. "Main course?"

"Swift Sword, Johnson." Vagueness obviously irritated Hammermill.

Johnson's eyes darted around the crowded dining room. "Watch it, will you?"

Hammermill's thin mouth curled beneath his heavy mustache. "You looking for lip readers? Now who's paranoid?"

"The less said, the more secure, I presume." Johnson had enjoyed putting Hammermill off balance with the payment in the box. Ill-advised gamesmanship, perhaps, but he'd succumbed to the temptation to ruffle Hammermill's insufferable superiority. Yet Johnson found himself equally as jumpy when Hammermill responded in kind. His conversational use of the term "Swift Sword" had brought the acrid bile of alarm into Johnson's throat. "You know what to do now," he said in an effort to regain composure. "Report to me when you've done it."

"I don't 'report.' I'll inform you." Hammermill's piercing black eyes speared him. Dark eyes were supposed to inspire trust, Johnson had read. Damned if Hammermill's didn't instill something cold and worrisome. Did they truly have the right man for the job?

"Who else on your side knows about the operation?" Hammermill asked.

"Just one other. The party initiating and funding it."

"Just the one?"

Johnson nodded and resumed his fiddling with the silverware. "That's what makes it so beautifully controllable."

"It will be from my end. It damned well better be from yours. If it blows, you're going down with me."

A useless threat, Johnson thought. If Swift Sword went awry, nobody involved would be coming back out of it, including Hammermill. That was the only comforting aspect of the whole, delicate proposal, aside from the blood-pulsing excitement that he had enjoyed from the outset. Then Johnson had a disquieting thought.

Might Hammermill leave a small contract of his own behind, to be actuated if he failed?

When their lunches arrived, Johnson talked absently about the bleak January weather. The dining room was far from overheated, but dampness began to soak his undershirt as he wondered how he was going to leak to Roger Kinchlo with the security of anonymity and without the insecurity of widening the circle of those who needed to know.

Twenty-nine minutes later, Johnson dabbed his thin lips with his napkin, took a final swallow of coffee, then patted his mouth again—a gesture that Hammermill found irksome. He nodded at Hammermill, who offered an equally detached response. Then Johnson pushed back his chair, stood and threaded his way among the intervening tables to the cashier, paid the check for both of them, paused at the coat rack to shoulder into his gray chesterfield, then left without looking back.

Hammermill watched him out of sight without moving. Then he promptly followed. Not even the acutest observer, he was confident, would note the carefully maintained distance between them. Hammermill paused at the dining room's entrance. Through the glassed lobby exit doors, he could see Johnson in the parking lot. The tall go-between walked swiftly, bald head downcast, to his car. He bent to unlock the Pontiac's door on the driver's side. Cautious man, Hammermill noted, but not cautious enough. That business with the little gift-wrapped box had been a stupid piece of minor-league theatrics.

IIe had assumed that Johnson was no more than a paid liaison man for one of several possible embassies Hammermill knew to be deeply interested in the future of one Benjamin Sokolo. But Johnson's unexpected "GS-

12" quip had jarred that assumption. Was the man a plant?

Hammermill waited in the lobby until the metallic green Pontiac rolled toward the Interstate-270 access ramp. Then he trotted through the frigid drizzle to his dark blue Olds and followed the Pontiac into southbound traffic, allowing two cars to slip into the space between him and the comfortably paced Pontiac.

Sleet began to streak the light rain, clotting inbound D.C. traffic. Hammermill nearly lost his subject at the exit, where part of the increasingly heavy traffic split off to the right toward the Capital Beltway. Visibility was hampered by road film, despite his flailing windshield wipers. Then he spotted the Pontiac bending into Wisconsin Avenue. Barely in time, he swung to follow Johnson through Bethesda's clutter, then into the District.

So the man probably was not CIA. He would have taken the Beltway westward to the GW Parkway for an eastward swing into Langley.

FBI? Johnson hardly seemed the type. Too old, for one thing, unless he was senior management level. Justice Department? A possibility. The JD people weren't so easy to categorize.

Then the green Pontiac, now three cars ahead in the stop-and-go city traffic, led Hammermill across Massachusetts, which he considered a logical route to the FBI building and to the neighboring Justice Department. Now what? They passed the parklike expanse of the Naval Observatory grounds to the left, then rolled into Georgetown. Now Johnson snaked a convoluted route east on P Street and somehow emerged on the Rock Creek Parkway. Then he cut suddenly into Virginia Avenue. Did the man sense or even realize he was being tailed?

Virginia Avenue angled into Constitution a half-dozen blocks from here, another way to the Justice Department. Hammermill had the guy tagged, and in the closed car, he felt a sudden spurt of hot nervousness. He stabbed the vent control. Was it possible that Johnson's touches of amateurish ineptness were a cover, part of an intricate Justice Department trap?

Then Hammermill got a surprise. The Pontiac had disappeared. He swiveled his head frantically. Lost the son of a bitch right here on wide open Virginia!

No, there he was, swinging off to the right, into a massive building that Hammermill recognized with a jolt to the stomach.

Johnson's Pontiac had turned into the huge building bounded by Twenty-first and Twenty-third streets and C and E streets and brushed on its northeast corner by angling Virginia Avenue. The U.S. Department of State.

4

CHARLIE LOVETT, *NewsLeak's* managing editor, was two hundred pounds of loosely connected flab with a collapsed face and crest of meringue. He'd taken the job as a presumably easy coast into retirement when Markelhenny outlined his concept for an American tabloid, *NewScope,* as it was initially called.

Assemble a crew of rewrite aces to redo wire service stuff with a flash of T&A, a dash of gore, and a flair for the bizarre. The balance would come from digging through available sources—Ripley, if they had to—and from freelancers.

On top of that, the rag was to be a biweekly. None of the pressure of the upstate daily Charlie had lately found so burdensome. A nine-to-five glide, and so it had been until Forrest, of all people, had turned creative.

Charlie had taken on Dan Forrest at Dan's solemn word that he was permanently dry. There had been times thereafter when Charlie had wished Dan would maybe knock one back and mellow out a little. The guy took his work too damned seriously. The hotshot re-

28

portage that had been bottled up—that was a good one!—through all those blown years was boiling out now. Forrest was, what? Forty-odd, and he'd turned into a checkout Jack Anderson, for corn sake. After Dan's Florida thing, Markelhenny had rethought his U.S. tabloid venture and sent word from Cardiff to change its name from *NewScope* to what some Welsh marketing genius told him was the far more saleable name, *NewsLeak. NewsLeak!*

And the budget for crime-prying was goosed. Also goosed, Charlie promptly discovered, was the pressure on him personally to produce. The paper was still primarily a rewrite op, but now the Cardiff Giant expected creative lead stories to wrap around the pap. "Peach Pits Can Kill" wouldn't do it alone anymore. Now such regurgitated revelations were to be led into the supermarket circulation clashes with banners the likes of, "*NewsLeak* Reporter Severs Vengeance Chain." Which 72-point head had indeed appeared in the wake of Forrest's impetuous Gulf Coast killer chasing. It had, in fact, precipitated Markelhenny's current blood-lusting and made Charlie's once comfortable cynosure into a real job.

Some real job. The biweekly publication schedule did them out of spot news coverage. The stuff came over the press wires red hot, but *NewsLeak* wasn't able to do much with breaks that hit after the damned twice-a-month deadline, except chew it over in the next issue. That was only one of the problems bugging Charlie Lovett. Now his crime man was hopping up and down over a Hollywood heartbreak story, when the rest of the country was waiting to find out just what Washington planned to do about the Penn Station thing.

Still, there wasn't much percentage in putting Forrest back on that one. It was a day-to-day story. Anything

NewsLeak could do with it would be a dead gosling by the time the tab next went to press. So titillating feature stuff had to be it, not hard news—except when luck struck. Charlie found himself hung up between a demand that was more than he'd signed on for and the frustration of a publication schedule that forced the rag to pass up news breaks.

All of which Charlie suffered as a chronic pain in the neck. This morning, the pain was moving southward fast, as he gazed across his trashed desk at Corkie Brion's set chins and Dan Forrest's folded arms. Lousy body language for a rainy winter morning.

"It's a celebrity story," Corkie insisted, "and that makes it my department."

"Crime," Dan pointed out, "is mine."

"Accidental death is not a crime, my dear. Tell him, Charlie."

Their harassed editor ran his hand across his rubbery face. Corkie's and Dan's stares stayed in sharp and stomach-souring focus. "What makes you think crime is involved here?" he asked Dan.

"Detective Leroy Forrest."

"Your cousin Roy?"

"My cousin Roy. I know his technique, Charlie. He's been ordered to lay off, but he's not convinced. So he wants to use me."

"You don't mind being used?"

"It could get Markelhenny what he wants."

"You think foul play is invol—"

"Oh, Lord, Charlie!" Corkie burst out. "Talk modern idiom. The woman wasn't beat up. The woman wasn't screwed. The place wasn't burgled. No crime, only that weird ritual stuff."

"So isn't that enough right there? We'll go with that."

They both went at him. He held up his hands. "Holy Hannah, you two! One at a time."

"It can be a big one, Charlie. My first shot at the front page." Corkie's eyes glittered. *"Top Box Office Draw Is Victim of Obscure Sex Practice.* My God, it's beautiful. But I've got to get more background, big names, who she was going with, Hollywood reactions—"

"Charlie," Dan broke in. "Roy thinks it's more than that, but he's been officially muzzled for no apparent reason. Even if we get his okay to break it, do you want to throw this story away as a one-shot celebrity sex kink thing?"

"All right! All right!" Charlie wished to hell they'd both go back to their cubicles and grind out what they were supposed to grind out. But, damn it, here was Markelhenny hanging over his shoulder as ominously as if he were in the room. "Jeez, Corkie, if you didn't already have a story to file, I'd—"

"It's on my desk, Charlie. Finished. The whole Mendenhall Pictures scam, ready to print."

"With names?"

"Big names, Charlie. You'll be stunned, shocked, and titillated."

"You leveling?"

"Never leveler. And I'm not thinking of a bonus."

"Good nonthinking."

"I'm thinking of . . . You know what I'm thinking of."

Charlie threw up his arms. "Ah, hell. All right, you *both* have it. Work together. I don't care how. Just come up with a story that sells papers. You got me?"

That shut them up. A stroke of genius, Charlie retrospected. Why hadn't he thought of this ten minutes ago? He plunked into his squealing swivel and plowed into the landfill on his desk. Then he looked up.

"You hear me? What is it, shell shock that you're going to have to work together?"

Dan's voice sounded parched. "Are you telling me to collaborate with this . . . this rip and rewrite artist?"

Charlie swung his shirt-sleeved arms wide in exasperation. "Kee-rist! We're *all* rip and rewrite artists here, Dan. That's *NewsLeak's* national image. Departmental niceties are not the issue. Copy that competes on the rack is the issue. So get the hell out of here, both of you, and, since you don't believe the police report, get moving on just what did happen to one Marguerite Falkenham."

"Falconer," Corkie amended.

"Whatever. You think it's more than autoerratic whatchamajummy, go ahead and prove it."

It wasn't so much Corkie Brion personally. It was his being forced to work with one of the Muses. He and Quince Harris, the paper's general feature writer and token youth, and even caustic arts reviewer Jonathan Blauvelt considered the Three Muses as no more than a hackney factory of flyweight fillers, not always inert, but hardly ever newsworthy. Now Dan was about to have corpulent Corkie pilot fishing along on a tip—well, an implied tip—from no less than Cousin Roy. This same Cousin Roy routinely growled warnings to Dan to stay off his NYPD turf. But this time, Roy had been waved off his own case, and Dan had become the recourse. Unique, to say the least.

"I hear, dear boy," Jonathan said in Dan's open cubicle doorway, "that you and Corkie are a thing."

"Good news travels fast."

32

Blauvelt smoothed the thigh of his black wet-look plastic trousers and cocked a salmon-draped elbow. "No hope there. She's a piece of the rock."

"You've tried? Have you, at long last, no decency, sir?" Blauvelt's exploitation of *NewsLeak*'s sparse female roster in the guise of a sexual agnostic was office legend.

"As she herself said, we won't go into that." The arts critic peered down the corridor, then smirked. "I think you've reaped the whirlwind, Daniel. She's already heading out."

"What!" Dan shoved past him and caught Corkie's arm at *NewsLeak*'s tawdry corridor entrance. "Time for a meeting."

"I don't need a meeting. I'm on my way."

"Charlie said together, damn it. I can't have you running all over town on your own."

"Who can't?"

"I . . . We can't. Come on, take off your trenchcoat and get yourself up to my cubicle."

"Mine," she said.

"Oh, hell. Wait a minute, then. I'll get my own coat, and we'll go to Oscar's."

They emerged from the dismal rain into coffee and grease aromatics a half-block distant. Neutral ground. The booth was plywood, stained crankcase oil brown, cushionless and scarred. The coffee Dan brought from the counter that ran down one side of the railroad-carlike eatery needed a lot of sugar, but Corkie's four ladles of it did seem a tad excessive.

"All right, now." He pointed his spoon at her for emphasis. "You don't like the way this has shaped up. I don't like it. But here's how we're—"

"Who," she asked, pointing her own spoon, "appointed you boss?"

"Damn it, somebody has to be in charge, just so we won't fall over each other checking the same leads."

She lowered the spoon. "A point. You have any?"

"Points?"

"Leads."

"Not yet." He lifted his clunky mug. "You?"

"I thought I'd start at the theater where she was appearing."

He shrugged. "Obvious."

"Then why didn't you suggest it?"

"Ah, hell. Let's both go up there."

She slid two quarters across the yellowed Formica.

"What's that for?"

"My coffee, partner. I pay my way."

They split the taxi fare, too, then stood inhaling its departing monoxide blat under the dripping icicles that fringed the marquee of the theater on West Forty-fourth.

"You can do the talking," she said generously. He wondered about that, because show biz was her beat. When they got past the rent-a-cop in the lobby, felt their way down the darkened aisle, and he spoke to the first guy in the little group in the third row, he knew.

"Crap!" exploded the tiny man with the shiny bald skull and horn rims. "We're trying to put the pieces together for tonight. We don't need goddam reporters!"

He turned out to be, after Dan worked the words "possible police cover-up" into the discussion, Sol Fingerwold, the producer of *Turn up the Heat,* a venture at the moment seriously jeopardized by the behavior of Marguerite Falconer's understudy up there on the stage.

The two men on Fingerwold's far side looked like stockbrokers, hard-faced in the soft fallout of the stage lighting. One was lean and coldly mean-looking; the other, plump with a scalp reflecting the kliegs through silver strands. They had something in common in addition

34

to their banker's dark pinstripes. They had faces of identical ashen gray. Mr. Crane and Mr. Armistead, Sol Fingerwold grudgingly ID'd them. Armistead was the chubby one. They represented two groups of backers— "angels," Fingerwold said in a condescending way, as if Dan and Corkie might not be aware of the jargon. The two gray-faced money men were watching their clients' cash swirl down the drain.

Dan assumed that much from not more than a minute's worth of the female understudy's guppylike performance. Then she gargled, "I *can't*. . . . I just *can't!*" And she ran sobbing to exit stage left.

Sol Fingerwold tossed both stubby arms high in a peculiarly Charlie-like gesture and groaned, "Oy, shit!" The angels' reps sat paralyzed by imminent disaster.

The male lead, a tall, too-handsome blond with stark black eyebrows, turned toward the limbo beyond the footlights and gave a "not my fault" shrug. Rinaldo Patton, Dan had deduced via the playbill outside.

From the darkness on the other side of the aisle came a dry, "Take ten, Rinaldo."

Fingerwold cocked a thumb toward the dim figure in ghostly white shirt-sleeves. "Theo Barnstable, my director. Talk to him, not me. I hardly knew the woman."

"I'll take Barnstable," Dan said to Corkie. "You want to try Rinaldo?"

Barnstable, gaunt, in his mid-thirties, furled and unfurled a dog-eared script. His lank reddish hair badly needed a trim, but today, that had to be the last of his concerns. The first surely was the debacle he had just witnessed up there on the boards. It had left him limp and peculiarly defenseless.

"From *NewsLeak*? How bad can things get?"

"We're talking with people who knew her," Dan said.

"Why? It was an accident."

"Maybe not."

"Jesus! What do you mean by that?"

"That's what I'm trying to find out, Barnstable."

The director glared up at the now empty stage and sighed. "I should be— Damn, I should be—" He shook his head and turned back to Dan. "Hell. You asking about people who knew her or who, uh, *knew* her?"

"I mean anybody she knew well enough to see at home."

"Well, not me. Oil and water. Stars like her travel in different orbits from mere directors."

A twinge of something here, Dan wondered? "Any people connected with the play who might have been with her offstage?"

"What the hell are you after?" Both long-fingered hands wound the script kindling-tight.

"I'm after specifics. One could lead to another, then maybe to something. Maybe to nothing."

"It wasn't an accident?" Barnstable wasn't totally preoccupied with his production problems.

"I've got an open mind."

"You think somebody . . . somebody . . ." He didn't seem able to say it.

"What kind of social life did she have here in New York, Mr. Barnstable?"

"The theater is pretty much all-consuming, Forrest, did you say your name was? Not a lot of time for that sort of thing."

"What sort?"

"Extracurricular. Thought there were some stories."

"Stories?"

"More like comments. This is a bitchy business, and she was a beautiful woman."

36

"Could you stop waltzing and get down to it? She's dead. You can't hurt her now."

Barnstable looked at the tight cylinder he'd made of the script in his lap. "Only her memory."

"There's not a lot of sentiment left in the world. If there is anything with an aroma, the hyenas will soon be skulking."

"So I notice."

Dan sank into the aisle seat beside the freckled director. "I'll level with you, Barnstable. I think she was done in." To back that, he had only Roy's chagrin at being preemptorily called off, but a little enhancement couldn't hurt.

"You mean some son of a bitch—"

"Just between us guys," Dan said.

Barnstable turned his head ninety degrees to stare into Dan's noncommittal return gaze. "You might check out Rinaldo," the director said to end a long beat of silence.

Presumably, Corkie was doing just that.

"And Duncan Crane," Barnstable added.

That was a grabber. "The voice of angels, right over there?"

"The same."

"And that's it?"

"That's all I'm aware of. She'd only been here a couple of weeks. Flew in from the Coast for rehearsals before that. Moved here for a week of final rehearsal, and we've only been open five days."

"That's time enough to make more than two friends."

"We're not talking Miss Congeniality here. She was selective about who got to know her."

"To know her, or to *know* her?"

"To see her at home, Forrest." The seat flew back as Barnstable pushed to his feet like a man who'd just run a marathon. "That's all I've got time and energy for. You saw a star being miscarried when you came in? That's my overriding concern."

Dan moved into the aisle to let him pass. "You won't quote me, okay?" Barnstable urged.

"There wasn't anything to quote."

"So be it." The gaunt director walked to the chest-high footlights and called Rinaldo Patton out of the wings for a muttered consultation. By the time Corkie returned to the aisle, Dan had secured a business card from an apprehensive Duncan Crane.

"You get anything?"

"I got the idea that Rinaldo never got anything, if that's what you mean, Daniel. He says he was at her apartment a couple of times. The night she died, he got there as one of the show's backers was leaving."

"Crane?"

"Five points for you. Rinaldo said they had a drink, went over some script changes, then he left. So he claims. He also claims she was fine when he said good night around half past ten."

"You said he was there another time."

"A week ago. For a script conference with Barnstable and Fingerwold."

"Was he aware of any acquaintance of hers here who was beyond the air-kissing stage?"

"Rinaldo hinted."

"Oh?" They walked slowly up the aisle.

"I got the idea that he had ideas, but he was cut out by somebody else."

"Crane?"

"No, when he talked about Crane, his nostrils never flared."

"Rinaldo's a nostril flarer?"

"All of that." She pushed through the exit door, then held it for him. Reflex, no doubt. In the lobby, she said, "There were little flickers when I asked him if he knew of anybody else she might have known well enough to invite to an intimate evening at the Chelsea Carlisle."

"Nostrils?"

"If he'd had a hoof, he would have scraped the floor with it."

"But you didn't get a name?"

"He didn't know the name, Daniel."

"Next time I'd better stay with you."

"Why? To Mutt and Jeff the subject?"

"You know about that?"

"Oh, you're such an impulse buyer. Look beyond the apparent, will you? Fat girls can have brains. Next step?"

"The Chelsea Carlisle."

"The doorman."

"Very good. They didn't tell me about your lightning intuition."

She gave him a toothy stage smile. "They did tell me about your crocodile tenacity. No genius, they said, but he never lets up."

"Who said?"

"I never reveal a source, Daniel."

They stepped into the frigid rain. He splashed off the curb to snag a taxi.

O'Connell, his name was; a tall man with the fine silver fox features of aging Irish gentry. His burgundy uniform should have been tweeds topped with a crushable walking hat, not the Chelsea Carlisle's visored disc. They caught him on the house phone just inside the brass-framed plate glass.

"Whom did you wish to see, sir?"

"You, Mr. O'Connell." The name was engraved in script on the little brass pin over his right breast pocket.

O'Connell was not pleased to be visited by the press again. Third or fourth time today, he informed them crisply, and all wanting information he did not have—and would not supply if he had had it. Thus you, sir, and the lady were wasting your time and his.

"What we wonder about," Dan said, "is who might have visited Miss Falconer that particular night, the night she died."

"Indeed? The privacy of our tenants is paramount, Mr. . . . ah . . ."

"Forrest."

"Mr. Forrest."

"She's dead, Mr. O'Connell," Corkie said. "Not much can hurt her now."

"Her memory, miss."

"You're paid to guard that, too?"

O'Connell flicked a disdainful eyebrow at her. "I'm sure *you* understand, sir," he said to Dan.

"Certainly. You'll have to excuse my colleague. She's new at this. Inclined to be a little . . . carried away."

Corkie took the cue smoothly. "He's only a *doorman*, Forrest. Give him five or ten, and let's get the info."

"Really, miss! O'Connell's pink flush went nicely with his platinum temples.

"That's enough," Dan rapped. "Why don't you take a walk. Check traffic or something. Go on, you aren't needed here."

She sulked off, and O'Connell visibly relaxed.

"Sorry about that, Mr. O'Connell. There was no need for her to . . . Look, I can keep this confidential. And if there's a charity you'd prefer—"

"This is the Chelsea Carlisle, sir! There is no need for that sort of tawdry business. Excuse me a moment." He rushed across the carpeted foyer to open the exterior door, then the lobby door, for an incoming mink jacket. The wizened wearer smiled. O'Connell touched his visor.

"Miss Landstreet," he told Forrest. "Twelve years with us."

"You know them all?"

"Certainly."

"What about visitors?"

"We insist that they show identification and register on the sign-in/sign-out sheet here."

"Well, Mr. O'Connell, just between us, you understand, I've learned that the police aren't entirely certain that Marguerite Falconer did die from accidental causes. That's why the matter of visitors may turn out to be important."

The Corkie-inspired pink faded from O'Connell's high cheekbones, replaced by something close to pallor gray. "Are you talking . . . murder, sir?" He pronounced it "morder," the only hint, so far, of a carefully repressed brogue.

"Possible foul play," Dan managed with a straight face. "Tell me, Mr. O'Connell, what will it take to get a look at the sign-in sheet for the night of the fifth?"

The doorman peered at something indistinguishable across the street. "Morder," he mouthed softly. "My good God. Well," he said, his unfocused gaze suddenly snapping back to this side of Seventy-seventh Street, "you have already named the price. Keep my name out of it. The management would not appreciate notoriety on the part of its staff. I trust you will so inform your—" Here his lip visibly curled. "—your female assistant?"

41

Was it possible, Dan wondered, that he had run into the only service employee on the island of Manhattan who didn't have his hand out? "That, Mr. O'Connell, is a given."

Whereupon O'Connell flipped back several pages in the leather-bound register on his little desk in the foyer. "Here we are, sir. Not a very active evening. It seems just two people visited 1407 that particular night. A Mr. Duncan Crane at 8:10. He stayed not quite an hour. Next up was a Rinaldo Patton at 9:05. He signed out at 10:30."

And the time of death was midnight or after. "Were you on duty that evening, Mr. O'Connell?"

"My shift is from 8 A.M. to 4 P.M. There are two others, Mr. Clermont and Mr. Brickell. Three eight-hour shifts. Mr. Clermont would have been on at that particular time."

"How good is your security?"

"You mean, could someone get in without our seeing? Not very likely. The emergency exits and delivery entrance in the rear open only from the inside. One of us is always here at the main entrance. There just is no way."

"Unless maybe someone inside opened an exit door for someone outside."

"That would have been witnessed by a surveillance camera and acted upon by our security officers."

That was a revelation. "There's an electronic security system here?" Now Dan noticed the barely visible lens just above a towering palm in the lobby. "Where's the monitor bank?"

"Just off the mezzanine. Two officers are on duty at all times. All entrances are camera equipped."

So much for the inside job idea. "Any other access? The garage? I noticed the entrance halfway down the block."

"Did you also notice the sign that says PRIVATE, ADMISSION BY ACCESS CARD ONLY?"

"What's that mean?"

"It means you must have a specific plastic card with a coded magnetic strip that activates the gate when it is inserted in a slot at the entrance. There is no other way to open that gate to be let in or out."

"Couldn't someone just duck under the gate?"

"I hardly think so. The gate is not one of those simple wooden arms that swing up and down. It's a steel security grid, much like those that jewelers pull down at night across their entire storefronts. Hardly the kind of device one 'ducks' under."

O'Connell took obvious relish in details, formality, and form. Marks of the retired teacher, Dan guessed, supplementing an inadequate pension.

"Do you think it might be possible for me to get a look at the monitoring room?"

"Why?"

"To be able to report how secure this place is."

"I don't believe a brief visit would hurt at that. I'll tell Sergeant McMichaels you are on your way."

Not bad, O'Connell, Dan thought. That will keep me from wandering in any other direction. The doorman indeed had a responsible eye on things.

So did keg-chested McMichaels, a smallish man built without discernible slack and with a disproportionately long face. He wore law and order blue with yellow Mastiff Security Service shoulder patches that sported a dog's head logo. Below the twin patches were twin sets of three yellow chevrons.

"Mr. Forrest?" He moved aside to let Dan into security central, an impressive bank of black-and-white TV monitors, twenty-four of them stacked in four rows of six, and not much more: a desk, chair, coffee maker on a stand, couple of phones, and a tape-cassette file against the near wall, beneath a rack of functional-looking VCRs.

Dan didn't notice the second watchdog in a remote corner until McMichaels aimed a thumb at him. "Officer Jennings." Jennings was no mastiff; more of a basset, with his cap tilted back along with his chair, as he angled a thermos of something into a Styrofoam cup. Jennings nodded.

"It's all up there." McMichaels jacked his prominent chin toward the monitor bank. "One for each of the fifteen floors, one at each of the ground-floor entrances, one each per elevator, one covering the interior garage access door, two scanning the roof."

The fifteen floor cameras cycled ceaselessly through ninety-degree arcs to cover both halls on each L-shaped floor. The other cameras were fixed.

"You don't have one on the garage's vehicle entrance?"

"Got an indicator light up here and a buzzer. Then we watch the monitor on the garage-to-elevators door."

"Isn't that kind of an awkward setup?"

"Budget. The unit racks twenty-four monitors. A twenty-fifth would have called for a whole additional setup." McMichaels shrugged. "It's pretty damned foolproof, Forrest."

"You want to bet?"

"You some kind of expert?"

"I wrote a piece on residential security last year."

McMichaels snickered. "Writing about it is one thing. Busting a system is another."

44

"Maybe so." Dan nodded toward the cassette file. "You keep tapes of all these things?"

"For forty-eight hours. Then we recycle. They're stop frame, three-second intervals, otherwise we'd be up to our noses in cassettes."

"How about the tapes made the night of the accident?"

"The Falconer thing? We held those, but the cops never asked."

"You still got them?"

"Yeah." Jennings had finally come to life. "I been waiting for the sarge to tell me to get them back in the cycle."

"How about holding them a while longer?"

McMichaels gave Dan an unsettled look. "How much longer?"

"Through tomorrow? I'd be glad to pay . . . uh, a 'storage fee.'"

"We'll hold them. No 'fees,' Forrest."

Dan was reasonably sure there was nothing noteworthy on the tapes, which, by now, the bored security duo had surely reviewed. They would have been eager to blurt out a finding. Unless they'd been bought. But their refusal of his not-so-ambiguous "fee" offer seemed to establish the fact that the Chelsea Carlisle had managed to assemble something of a true-blue staff.

He had seen enough, thanked Sergeant McMichaels, and found Corkie in unexpected rapport with O'Connell just inside the front entrance. Apparently, the frostily formal doorman was susceptible to free coffee.

"Got it over there Chez Tante Giselle," she said when they were back in the rain. "A buck and a quarter a cup! This *is* a tony neighborhood."

45

"You do know about Mutt and Jeff. That was a quick take with O'Connell. You got him to hate you by barely lifting a lip."

"It's a talent. Got him back, too. What did you dig up in there?"

"They're overly proud of a security system you could drive a homicide through." He raised the collar of his drenched London Fog. Now the rain was streaked with sleet. "I'm going to try something. It might take a while. You want to wait or go back to the office?"

"Are you kidding? I'm coming with you."

"Too conspicuous."

"You never miss a chance, do you?"

"Too conspicuous with two, Corkie, not you specifically."

"I'll wait Chez Tante's, then. Maybe I can get a four-dollar hot dog."

He watched her cross Seventy-seventh toward the narrow little restaurant wedged between two hulking apartment buildings. In her billowing navy blue coat, she was impressively light-footed for a heavy woman.

Dan jammed his hands in his coat pockets and walked through the falling murk along the Chelsea Carlisle's south flank toward the garage entrance. This could be done in five minutes or stretch into the afternoon, but he was going to do it, no matter how long it took. For his own satisfaction, but particularly because he wanted to relish the expression on McMichael's overconfident face.

5

IT TOOK TWENTY MINUTES of constructive loitering in the
sleet, glancing at his watch, swinging his head up and
down the street in a stood-up-for-a-ride act, wishing to
hell he'd worn a hat, any kind of hat. The downfall was
ice granules now, salting his thin hair, and pricking his
scalp.

Then a pearl gray Olds turned into the garage and
stopped at the gate's lock post. The driver, a well-fed,
middle-aged man, slotted in his magnetically coded card.
The metal grid that spanned the entrance rolled upward
smoothly. The Olds burbled in. The gate automatically
began its metallic descent. Dan was inside before he had
to duck more than a few inches under the lowering
bottom rod.

He timed his approach to the red-painted interior
door to arrive just as the Olds driver did. With the
sometimes exaggerated courtesy of the moneyed, Mr.
Olds held the door for him.

"I thank you, sir," Dan said amiably, careful to keep his face averted from the nearby surveillance camera's eye. "Stevens. Andy Stevens. Just moved in."

"Edgar Markham. I trust you'll enjoy it here. Fine place."

Dan smiled briefly, walked past the emergency stairs to the elevators and stood impatiently with his hands behind his back to help Markham watch the flashing lights of the floor indicator. As one of the two cars arrived at garage level and its door slid open, Dan grunted. "Damn! Forgot my briefcase."

"I'll hold the elevator for you."

"Thanks, but my car's way over on the far side. I'll have to catch the next one." He walked back toward the garage access door, stopped when he heard the elevator door shut behind him, then began the long climb up the emergency stairwell.

Twelve flights of concrete steps would have been an attention-worthy climb for a serious jogger. Dan's occasional sprints to the subway didn't come close. The dozen flights to the fourteenth floor were murder. He was as damp inside the raincoat as was the weather outside when he cracked the exit door on floor fourteen. After a carefully timed pause, he rushed out of the stairwell and ran the length of the hall on protesting legs. Fourteen-oh-seven was just around the corner, fifteen feet down the other hall.

He stood at the door of 1407 for nearly six minutes before Sergeant McMichaels burst out of one of the elevators, beet-faced and sputtering, one stunned and outflanked Mastiff. "Friggin' wise ass," he growled. "Friggin' wise ass."

"Better tell the management to stop protecting the sacred budget," Dan suggested amiably, "and put some real money into tightening up this sieve."

On their way back to *NewsLeak*'s office, Corkie said, "You look damned pleased with yourself. Tell me how you ruined their day, Daddy."

He'd thought she would never ask. "One of their problems is that the system doesn't visually cover the garage vehicle entrance. They have no idea how many people are in an incoming car. I went through to the elevators talking with an arrival Security recognized, and they assumed I had come in with him. So their system is fatally flawed right there. Then there's not a damned thing in the stairwell, and the doors of each floor open from either side. The floor scanners cycle, and most of the time they're staring at nothing but the inside walls. No trick to beating that. If I could do it, anybody could. The tenants feel snug as rugged bugs, but the place is a public open house."

"So anybody with a touch of smarts could have gotten in and up to fourteen that night, then back out the same way."

"You got it."

"Or with the stairwell a two-way street, anybody already living there could have nipped up or down to fourteen-oh-seven unseen, then back down or up."

He stared at her as the taxi galloped across Fifth Avenue. "That, my dear Watson, is a dimension I hadn't considered."

Hammermill, as he currently called himself, worked out of unfancy digs in a Wheaton, Maryland, building that had seen better times—and better tenants. The Washington-Baltimore consultancy boom had begun with faceless erections of precast concrete in deteriorating Maryland farmland. Then the high-tech roll prompted office space construction with lobbies that impressed and with decor befitting what was rapidly becoming Silicon

Valley East between the two sprawling metro areas. The lure of such fancier footage left buildings such as Rathmussen Tower in the low-rent lurch, which suited J.B. Hammermill just fine.

He took a corner of the fourth floor at a rate he was able to negotiate downwards without much haggling. He employed as managing editor one Earl Rice, a recent grad of Bob Jones University. Rice looked clean, lived clean, and could spell, thus Hammermill shifted the main editorial load of *Red Alert* off his own back and onto Earl's.

The thing was a newsletter, made up each month of bits and scraps of ostensibly inside information on the Red Menace. Such items were gleaned from a tidal surge of incoming magazines, newspapers, reports from self-appointed informants, crank letters with occasionally literate bits that were reported in the "Unsubstantiated But Noteworthy" column, and reports irregularly sent in by several paid informants in certain strategic hot spots. The ceaseless culling was done by a fortyish and blowsy brunette carried on the masthead as Gladwyn Coski, Contributing Editor, known to *Red Alert's* staff— but to very few others—as Hammermill's wife. She was always careful to set aside for Hammermill's full perusal the reports for which he paid.

At the word processor, turning out the cold-type galleys to be rubber-cemented into the monthly paste-up, was an unusually tall Afro-Asian, half-Vietnamese–half-black American, named Francine Nguyen. She had taken her mother's name, because her mother was unaware of her father's name after an unexpectedly impregnating one-night stand in the back room of a Saigon bar.

Typing the galleys and preparing the mechanicals for the job press in Gaithersburg constituted two-thirds of Franky's services to J. B. Hammermill. The other third was personal and was undertaken only when Gladwyn was safely overwhelmed with her in-house clipping service and Franky called in sick. On such days, Hammermill took unusually long lunch hours.

He wondered if Gladwyn noticed the coincidences. She'd never shown an indication of any sort. He also wondered if Earl Rice had tied together the coordination of Franky's indispositions with some of Hammermill's longer lunches. No doubt that would offend the puritannical values that had surely been a heavily stressed part of BJU's curriculum. But Earl said nothing either.

On the face of it, Hammermill had about assumed he could enjoy Franky's outside services indefinitely. Her talents in that area were infinitely more engaging than were the randy clutchings Gladwyn demanded not more than three or four times a month, thank God.

Franky was to Gladwyn as Bristol Cream was to raw gin, Hammermill mused, as he lay comfortably naked on his back in the overheated motel room, while sleet pecked at the picture window behind the closed drapes.

"This you like?" she murmured as an electric shiver zipped from her silky fingers straight up his spine. He tried to anchor his concentration elsewhere.

With thirty-seven thousand subscribers, most of them with a remunerative 1950s mindset, *Red Alert* was almost at break-even. The contract mailing house and subscription fulfillment house in Arlington strove mightily to goose the circulation ever upward, and Hammermill made certain that Franky Nguyen and Earl Rice were ignorant of the well-concealed fact that *Red Alert* was a front. Only Gladwyn necessarily knew that. J. B. Hammermill's true vocation, like his real identity, was safe with her. He knew she was in love with him and afraid of him at the same time, a combination of emotions that she had admitted to him was irresistibly stimulating to her menopausal hormones.

What Hammermill did professionally, aside from final editing of his newsletter, was consulting work. Packaging might have been a more accurate word. If a certain Central American regime had a requirement for unrest in a neighboring republic, it need only inform the proper attaché in its Washington embassy of the requirement. The attaché had only to get in discreet touch with Hammermill and agree on the fee. He thought of himself as a counterterrorist, because he worked only in the interest of right-thinking clients. If Castro or Ortega had sought his services, they would have been unable to substantiate the rumor that such services existed.

He admired T.E. Lawrence and Gordon Liddy; even had Liddy's mustache. He'd failed at holding his palm over a candle. Didn't last long enough to acquire more than a sooty smudge before nerve failed. Would he show up at an appointed street corner were one of his clients desirous of eliminating him? That Liddy claim, he fervently hoped, would never be put to the test. But damn it, he knew he was just as competent in what he did as was the man he admired.

When what had turned out to the the U.S. Department of State—or no less than a highly placed contact thereof—had reached him shortly after the Penn Station bombing, he had experienced a sine wave of emotion: initial euphoria, then cold sweat that the thing might be a trap, then a warm suffusion of confidence that an entrapping agency wouldn't dally around like this, finally the pounding blood of realization that if somebody'd had the guts to undertake such a proposed act fifty years ago, there might not have been a World War II.

The trouble was . . . Johnson. That man seemed about as reliable as Philippine election results. A problem potential, if not immediate. Leave it to a D.C. bureaucracy to use a guy like that. This noon, Hammermill worried about Johnson's part in Swift Sword as he laced his fingers behind his head and gazed up at the swirled fibers of the motel's ceiling tiles. Concentration on the Johnson aspect was rapidly becoming difficult under the ministrations of Franky's eely fingers.

Falconer could have been trouble, according to Johnson. There was irony for you. But Hammermill had handled that easily enough through Thorp. Thank God for people like Thorp, the terminator doll. Wind him up, and he kills somebody. So the New York loose end had been tied, much too quietly in Hammermill's judgement. But that was Johnson's concern now. Hammermill's need was to get on with the project. He had made initial contact with Woodman across the river. That would be firmed into a specific order. Ingram M-20s should be excellent. Thirty-two-round magazines. The list price the last time he'd needed Ingrams was under $150 each.

As for personnel— He twitched. "Oop, Franky! You've got a hell of a touch." As for personnel . . . Her dexterity had teased him right to the jittery edge. The recruiting, damn it, had better begin within . . . within . . .

"You sly little devil!" He swung toward her, scrambled over her. She swarmed up around him. Maybe Uzis if he couldn't get Ingrams. . . . Easier to—

Then he was drowned in her heat, in soft bronze skin gliding on his sunlamp tan. Demand, demand, everybody wanted something. Made the world go around. He flew over the shattered rim of physical control and whirled down a velvet funnel. This was the part that always scared him a tad, the momentary, but total loss of self-possession. Threaded through the erotic whirl, he heard her little cries.

He struggled back, gazed down into her huge brown irises, touched the Oriental tucks at the inner corners of the half-closed eyes, the snubby nose, and glistening full lips.

"You love me, Jimmy?" Just a little tongue catch on the "l."

"Of course I love you."

She squirmed suggestively beneath his weight. "You lie. You love nobody but Jimmy. You use, not love people. You want to use me again?"

"Appreciate your faith, but I've got things to do." He freed her reluctantly. In the shower he suddenly realized that today was Thursday, and he always took Gladwyn out on Thursdays. When they returned to their Chevy Chase apartment, she routinely had demands of her own. He'd told Franky about that.

"You conniving little wildcat," he said when he came out of the stall toweling himself. "Did you pick Thursday on purpose?"

She was sitting on the edge of the bed, still without a stitch on, and she reached out to fondle him gently beneath the draped towel. "Why do you keep her, Jimmy, when you can have me? You did promise."

Yeah, he'd promised, all right. Anything to get this copper-skinned honey between the sheets. Trouble was, she remembered every damned thing he'd said to her, and she believed it all. He had become adept at putting her off with more promises—and two raises—but by now she expected a lot more than that. She'd gotten too damned possessive, and she figured she had him by the nuggies. Maybe she did, for the moment. But she was human Kleenex, as disposable as anyone else who reverted from asset to threat.

54

His eyes flicked across her taut little breasts with their large purple areolas, down her flat, smooth belly, to the ebony juncture of the golden thighs. Hell of an asset still. But she'd better watch her mouth.

"Get your clothes on." He'd had her, so now the hell with her. He needed to prioritize Woodman to begin building the strike team.

"Jimmy, if Gladwyn was to find out that we—"

He turned on her savagely. "God damn it! If there's anything I can't abide, it's a threatening woman! You keep your face shut or I'll shut it for you, *you hear me?*"

A fool thing to say, he realized immediately. "Hey, Franky!" He forced a grin and trailed his fingers playfully across the velvety skin of her breasts. "Get dressed, okay? I'm just a grumpy old man."

She reached for her panties, but the fear didn't leave her eyes.

Casey's call interrupted Dan and Corkie in mid-list. "Miss me?"

He did indeed, but "Damned right!" was all he managed with Corkie's inhibiting bulk pacing the kitchen side of his living room with the computer list down at waist level. He'd told her she ought to give in to glasses. All that got him was something unmistakably disparaging between a sneer and a snarl. Hell with her.

"How's Texas?"

"Lonely, Dan, with only a CRT to keep me warm." It was that kind of wistful conversation. He hung up and turned reluctantly from the memory of Casey's auburn-haired litheness to Corkie's bulk. The celeb writer stayed absorbed in the computer run-out that had been supplied none too graciously by Chelsea Carlisle management.

"You find anything?"

"Seventy-nine of the dullest, overmoneyed tenants ever assembled under one exorbitantly priced roof. You sure this list was worth exchanging for your promise not to blow their Swiss cheese security system?"

"They thought so. I'm under oath to that pompous manager of theirs not to release it or copy it and to return it tomorrow."

"Trusting soul, he."

"For all the good it's doing us. They're just names to me."

"Backbone of democracy," she murmured. "Quiet money. They— Hey, wait just a minute!"

Dan set down the coffee mug he'd just picked up. Corkie's ponderous presence was driving him to three cups a night, but there was no civilized way around her neighborliness, when her door opened directly across the hall from his.

"Something?" he prompted.

"Mr. and Mrs. Willard T. Holley, Junior. Fifteenth floor."

"The *mayor* lives there?"

"His son, Daniel. Junior. Ha-ho!"

"Ha-ho?"

"Just remembered. Willard Junior is noted for certain proclivities, all of them being female and noteworthy."

"A star chaser."

"Exactly that. I believe that I will have a chat with Willard tomorrow, if he's available. Care to string along?"

She had a knack of taking charge with a single phrase. "You play with Willy, if you want to. I'm going for the top money."

"Duncan Crane."

"Precisely. Appointment at ten."

Which he kept promptly. More than he could say for Crane, who kept him studying the mellow paneling of the third-floor lobby for twenty-one minutes before the finishing school brunette receptionist led him down the earth-tone carpeted corridor.

Duncan Crane obviously believed that the clients of Crane Associates, Financial Advisors, needed the reassurance of baronial office decor. His sanctum sanctorum's ceiling was lofty enough to encourage clouds. A mullioned picture window behind his half-acre desk offered a panorama of lower Broadway with the New York Stock Exchange prominent to the left. The view was interrupted only by the admirallike figure of Duncan Crane himself, seated in his tall sienna brown executive chair. He didn't get up, merely flicked a forefinger at a complementary rosewood chair on the desk's nearside, and nodded dismissal at Ms. Private School and her clinging beige knit sheath.

Crane, in three-piece charcoal—what else?—gave Dan's exhausted raincoat an appraising glance. "I can see you're not here to discuss investments, Mr. Forrest, was it? I can't imagine any other subject we might have in common."

Harvard or Yale? He had the attitude. And the finely shaped head with its weekly appointment hair trim and precise banker's salt-and-pepper part. The only crack in the ice cap demeanor was a tiny tic that persisted in lifting the left corner of Crane's slash mouth in a near subliminal flicker of disdain.

"What we have in common," Dan said, "is Marguerite Falconer." He watched the tic closely.

The man was either damned good at deadpan maintenance or he was babe innocent. The gray eyebrows didn't even hike.

57

"As I understand it, Mr. Forrest, you are flailing around for a story on Miss Falconer's unfortunate accident. Judging by the paper you work for, it's not going to be a tribute."

"According to the visitors' log at her apartment house, you visited her that night."

Crane tented his fingertips. "You've gone that far, have you? I'm not surprised. Yes, I was there to discuss a business matter with Miss Falconer. Concerning the play."

"The play?"

"I suppose there's no harm now in telling you. She wanted to invest in a piece of it. Since we were not fully subscribed, her interest was something of a financial godsend. Otherwise, we would have been betting against future ticket sales, a practice potentially more disastrous than borrowing against accounts receivable."

"She did buy a piece of the play that night?"

Crane dipped his patrician head and raised his eyes to Dan's, an oddly coy gesture. "She did, indeed. I took her the papers, she signed them on the spot."

"How did she seem at the time?"

"You mean emotionally? Delighted, elated. Apparently, she had never before owned an interest in a stage property."

"Not like somebody contemplating—" What could he call it, Dan wondered? "Contemplating a rash act?"

"That's an odd question. What kind of rash act?"

Okay, Crane, here goes. Roy has asked only that he not be personally implicated. "A sexual form of playing at suicide, only she apparently went all the way."

Duncan Crane's face drained near-white. "But the papers, the TV said it was an accident. Suicide? Outlandish suicide? That's impossible!"

58

"You don't understand the practice, Mr. Crane." As Dan explained it, Crane's fingers whitened on the arms of his expensively upholstered chair.

"God," he rasped. He cleared his throat. "She couldn't have been . . . like that. She had men. We, uh, investigated."

"We?"

Henry Armistead and I, before we took on the joint underwriting of *Turn up the Heat* for Fingerwold. We weren't about to raise seven figures for a dramatic venture with an unstable lead."

"And you learned—?"

"We ascertained that Marguerite Falconer had what could be considered a . . . well, a fairly active love life for a divorced woman of her age. Notably— Does all this have to go into your scandal sheet, Mr. Forrest?"

"I'm the crime reporter, not the celebrity sex kinks writer." One way to promise nothing at all.

"She occasionally had brief affairs with her leading men. Not consistently; she was selective."

"With Rinaldo Patton?"

"How would we know? The play just opened. In the past, she had been linked romantically with Harry Harrison, Colby Thatcher, Philip Doregan—all of them actors she had made movies with. Transient affairs. You could even term them recreational. I understand that sort of thing is common in Beverly Hills circles. Then there were a few names outside the business. Just a few. Zandy Keane was one of them. Edwin Stanfield was another."

Crane stopped, obviously bemused by Dan's lack of recognition. The corner of his mouth went tic, tic, tic. Then he relented. "Keane is . . . was Miss Falconer's stockbroker in Los Angeles. Attractive man. I suppose their frequent contact naturally led to a more intimate liaison. Stanfield was something of a surprise. He's an Under Secretary of State."

"In Washington?"

"Where else? Apparently, she met him at a reception at the Japanese Consulate in Los Angeles several months ago. There were rumors that she'd seen him again, when she appeared at the Indian Embassy in Washington to promote what has turned out to be her last film."

"*Soul of the Ganges.*"

"The Stanfield liaison—the alleged Stanfield liaison—was strictly rumor."

Stanfield. He had heard that name before. But in what connection? "Anybody else?" Dan pressed.

"We're not talking about an alley cat here, Mr. Forrest. She was a beautiful, idolized woman. It's . . . it was inevitable, I suppose, that her demanding lifestyle developed needs that the rest of us might find, well, somewhat flamboyant."

"Including the business of the rope in the bathtub?"

"That, sir, I find totally out of context with our precommitment investigation. She was a . . . lusty woman, if you will. Full of life, perhaps somewhat sexually demanding, but nothing in our discreet, but quite thorough, inquiries indicated any hint of perverse practices whatever."

Crane slapped his palms on his desktop and abruptly stood. The interview was over. He must have managed to touch a hidden button in the process because Ms. Private School quietly appeared in the doorway to escort Dan outbound.

"A final point," Duncan Crane called after him. "You do protect your sources, do you not? I much prefer not to have my name appear in a paper with a name such as *NewsLeak.*"

60

A neatly hypocritical afterthought, Dan felt, from a source who enjoyed gossip as much as had Mr. Duncan Crane.

He met Corkie for lunch at a chaotically crowded deli on Sixth. He heard her before he spotted her forging through the mob like a persistent tugboat.

"Dan! Dan! It's—" The rest of her shout was swallowed in the noontime din of the place. A lousy pick for a meeting.

"The *Daily News*—"

"Salami on pumpernickel, slice of dill!" shouted a beery voice in his ear.

"What?" Dan yelled at her. "What?"

"Kinchlo's column." She shoved the folded paper in his face. "Take a look. While we've been banging around town, the bastard's got it all!"

6

DAN READ IT on their fast walk back to the office. The sleet had faded to a sprinkle that spattered the tabloid where Dan scanned Roger Kinchlo's column, "The Lowdown."

WEIRD TWIST IN FALCONER DEATH!

The death of stage and screen star Marguerite Falconer turns out to be a shocking "accident" extraordinaire indeed, according to highly placed sources.

The internationally acclaimed golden-haired actress apparently was the victim of an exotic sex practice known as autoerotic asphyxia. This is a horrifying ritual in which the practitioner brings on a state of sexual rapture by choking him or herself just short of the point of death.

Unfortunately, it appears that Marguerite Falconer was not able to release the silken cord around her delicate neck in time. So she died. The family has requested privacy at her funeral, to be held today in her grieving hometown of Chicago. But many luminaries of the stunned world of show business are expected to attend. No doubt the media will have their customary field day.

Kinchlo wasn't having such a bad day himself with his "weird," "shocking," "exotic," and "horrifying" stops pulled.

"This strike you as a little odd?" Dan asked Corkie, who was trotting beside him through the postlunch midtown crowd.

"That the *News* has it before us? It's a daily. We're biweekly. Crippled in the starting gate."

"I mean that Kinchlo has it. He's West Coast, syndicated in the *Daily News.*"

"And a hundred other papers. It's a Hollywood story, isn't it?"

"Damn it, Cork, it happened *here,* and it's been under wraps. Somebody inside had to get to him. I wonder just who?"

"And maybe why?"

"Yep, and maybe why. You learn anything from Holley Junior?" Dan ducked around an oncoming trio of leather jackets and lank hair. Corkie forged right through them without breaking her choppy stride.

"I learned he's one scared puppy. Want details?"

"Wait 'til we get to the office. I'm running out of wind." She had a truck's stamina. He didn't catch his breath until they rode the rickety cage to *NewsLeak's* offices.

When the two of them crowded into her cubicle, Dan hunched on the corner of her desk, still breathing hard. Corkie, despite her proportions, looked as if she could have gone another couple of Manhattan miles. "I knew I'd hit some kind of payoff button," she said. "I knew it when all six feet of Willard T. Holley, Junior, turned into jelly, and he whimpered, 'I thought this had been hushed up.' "

She had tracked him down at Metro Motors, where he was a car salesman.

"A car salesman?"

"Jaguars and Lancias. The whitest of collars." At first, he had bluffed. He didn't even know Marguerite Falconer. How could he possibly be involved in any way with what had happened? Corkie had pushed him hard; finally promised not to implicate him. "Against all my, hah, principles, Daniel. But it was that or trying to pry meat out of a clam."

In his plush little deal-closing office off the showroom, Holley had then shut the door and slumped into the chair behind his brochure-strewn desk. That was when he'd come out with his whine about the thing's supposed to have been hushed up.

"He's a good-looking hunk," Corkie threw in. She said she could believe Holley and Falconer were something more than nodding acquaintance tenants when Falconer was in occasional residence for East Coast TV and theater work, which were the reasons she maintained the apartment.

"I gathered that, when Mrs. Holley was out of town on Junior League business—she's on the national board— and Falconer was in town on show business, they managed a fair amount of monkey business. He would drop down the stairwell and slide through the fourteenth floor's surveillance camera cycle for recreational purposes."

"He *admitted* that?"

"As much as. But he swears he didn't go near her apartment that night."

"You believe him?"

"What can be wrong with a man who sells Jags, Daniel? Besides, he said his wife was in residence that particular night and could corroborate his fireside presence all evening. Of course, he hoped to hell it wouldn't come to that. Apparently, he and Falconer had a long if sporadic relationship. He certainly knew she was seeing other men between times, so jealousy is hardly a motive. I'd say it was an arrangement of simple convenience for both of them. Uncomplicated and therapeutic."

"You got him to go into that kind of detail?"

"In as many words. I can believe him. He's a bit of a wimp, but for that health club bod of his, I could put up with a lot of wimpery. It would even be reassuring that he wouldn't have the fire to raise a fuss over whatever else I might do. Yes, I can believe that kind of a relationship with Falconer. Why is it so surprising that women go on the prowl, too?" She shrugged off her own question. "Oh, hell, it was a useless interview."

"You've missed the significance, Cork."

"What significance?"

"The reason the lid was put on. How's this: Holley Junior ulps when he hears something fatal has happened down on fourteen. Such news travels fast in little closed communities like the Chelsea Carlisle. A probe of Falconer's life-style would inevitably throw a loop around Holley Junior's wandering ankle, and God only knew where Mrs. Holley would run with it."

Dan shifted his butt on the hard desk. "So he phones Mayor Dad. The mayor isn't so taken with the adverse publicity possibilities either. He checks with his police commissioner. Circumstances at the scene being what they are, the PC is urged to put the clamps on. The medical examiner gives the PC his out. An accident. The media are so informed. No need to go into irrelevant exotic details. The lid stays on those. Holley Junior's public virtue—and marriage—are intact, and all's right with his and Dad's world."

"Neat, Daniel, but what about this?" She slapped the battered copy of the *Daily News* on her desk.

"That's the fly in the celebration champagne, Cork. It doesn't compute." He slid off the desk. "I've got to make a phone call."

"You think Roger Kinchlo will actually tell you who his source is?"

He looked back, a touch jolted. "Sometimes you scare me, kid. I dunno. But I'm going to try."

Under Secretary for Departmental Affairs Edwin Stanfield was pleased to see that the State Department's press room was crowded with far more members of the media than a routine briefing would have attracted. This was not a routine briefing. The spokesman, usually smiling old shoe Davis Rylander, was today to be the chief, himself: Secretary of State G. Thomas Bowlder. He didn't handle press briefings often. That was one reason for the boosted attendance. Another reason, obviously, was the subject of today's special appearance by Bowlder: the message from Nandia's President, Benjamin Sokolo, concerning the Penn Station massacre.

The gabble of the crowd died as Bowlder, elegant in a gray pinstripe, strode from a side entrance to the podium, with Stanfield close behind and Rylander trailing by several paces. Stanfield resented Rylander's little incorrigible laxities, but what could you expect from a TV anchor turned department chief spokesman? Bowlder took his place, standing behind the podium with its modest State Department seal. Stanfield and Rylander seated themselves at the far end of the first row, up front, yet dismissed by the press as window dressing minions. Just as well. Rylander's casual haberdashery would have contrasted badly with the formality of the stylized blue and yellow world map behind the narrow speaker's stand. He perpetually looked like a visiting time salesman from a minor radio station, Stanfield thought. The man actively resisted the unofficially approved three-piece somber suits that Bowlder favored and that went so well with the podium's background decor. Today Rylander wore a blue tweed sports jacket, a powder blue shirt instead of State Department white, and a rebellious red tie.

Stanfield himself was a model of subdued elegance in tailored charcoal. Elaine had told him on their second date that he looked like a dark-haired, hazel-eyed Paul Newman. "You're a little carried away," he said, but he was pleased, never forgot it, and it helped compensate for his middling stature. At fifty-eight, he still had his hair styled and blow-dried on alternating Thursdays.

"Good morning, gentlemen," Bowlder offered as a pro forma attention focuser. "And ladies," he added with an ingratiating smile. "I have a brief statement, then I will be glad to take questions."

He self-consciously smoothed his combed-back iron-gray hair with a palm, then extracted a single sheet of typing paper from a breast pocket and unfolded it. Bowlder was a tall man with piercing gray-blue eyes, a narrow ridge of nose, and thin colorless lips—a hard man to caricature except for the aggressive jut of his chin. He had FDR's jaw.

The secretary of state read his statement without glasses. He needed glasses, but he hated them. Only Stanfield, Rylander, and Bowlder's executive secretary knew the statement had been typed in huge Orator typeface.

"As you are aware, the Pennsylvania Railroad Station in New York City was the target of a terrorist bombing in mid-December. At 9 A.M., Eastern Standard Time today, this government received a cable from President Benjamin Sokolo of the West African Peoples Republic of Nandia. Mr. Sokolo expressed regret concerning the bombing, the three deaths, and the twenty-eight injured persons, and he acknowledges—repeat, he acknowledges—that the perpetrators were Nandian nationals in the United States on student visas."

A stir swept the auditorium, although Sokolo's cable had only confirmed what the State Department had known from the outset and what the press had assumed. Bowlder had been reading the statement in his familiar flat tone, but in his next words, Stanfield detected an emotional tautness that didn't quite carry over the sound system. The under secretary himself had considerable difficulty maintaining the protectively bland expression he had determined to wear throughout this briefing. Behind it, he was seething.

"Mr. Sokolo states that the bombing was undoubtedly a reaction to last year's United States embargo on continued economic aid to his country. He further states that he may not be able to prevent further similar reactions by the more radical elements of Nandians abroad. That is the extent of his statement—and of mine, ladies and gentlemen. I will now take questions."

An unintelligible barrage of shouts burst across the room. Stanfield turned to gaze into the turmoil, squinting against the TV lighting. He had to raise a bit from his chair to see over the press pack. His modest stature held him to a slight disadvantage among the impressively lofty types State seemed to prefer. He found face-to-face discussions with towering Secretary Bowlder to be awkward, and consistently hoped Bowlder would conduct them sitting down.

68

The secretary held up both hands to quell the undisciplined outburst. "Please, please! One question at a time." He shot out an arm. "Mr. Spence?"

The shouting subsided as Knight-Ridder's cadaverous Jack Spence stood. "Mr. Secretary, are we planning any sort of retaliation for this appalling act, anything along the lines of former President Reagan's reprisal raid on Libya, in response to Mr. Sokolo's incredible attempt at international extortion?"

"We are faced with a number of difficulties in formulating the proper response, Mr. Spence." Bowlder's formal statement had been straightforward, because Rylander had written it for him. Now, on his own, Stanfield noted, the secretary had lapsed into his characteristic stodgy convolutions. "There is the problem of pinpointed blame assessment, international policy consistency, and reaction containment. Effectuating an efficacious response is no simple undertaking. Mrs. Dikstraw?"

Emma Dikstraw, National Newsline Syndicate, was the only woman in the auditorium, possibly in the Middle Atlantic, who habitually wore a hat—a Bella Abzug derivative, no doubt intended, in this case, to conceal much of Dikstraw's graying hair. Her voice was high and tense. "Isn't retaliation a prerogative of the President, sir, and not the State Department?"

Bowlder contained his sudden flush to a mere inch rise above his snowy shirt collar. "Of course it is, Emma. I was simply trying to respond to the question." He pointed to a chunky man in dark green to the far left of the dais.

"Alvin Herlihy, *Chicago Tribune*. Mr. Secretary, might you give us your worst case scenario?"

Bowlder appeared perplexed.

"What I mean is, if a retaliation effort were to lead to a declaration of war by Mr. Sokolo—and I believe he in fact made such a threat last November—would this nation actually engage in military hostilities with Nandia?"

Bowlder's chin had taken on an aggressive jut. "My worst case scenario, Mr. Herlihy, would be the escalation of currently dormant high-level antipathy into active hostilities between this nation and, of course, the U.S.S.R. Nandia has become a Soviet client state. Mr. Sokolo now survives only because of Soviet logistical and economical underbracing. A confrontation between this nation and Mr. Sokolo could conceivably result in the eventuation of a negative vis-à-vis with the Soviets."

Stanfield groaned inwardly. The man was incapable of a simple declarative sentence, the result, no doubt, of his Groton-Harvard-corporate-law-firm experience chain. The under secretary, himself a product of Baltimore's Polytechnic High School, the University of Maryland, and its law school, then the prosecution side of the law, resented Bowlder's background, his elegance, even his damned Boston accent.

An inherited family trust could have seen Stanfield through a more prestigious educational stratum, but he early on had exhibited a streak of perversity that his Roland-Park-born and -bred father deplored. No easy way for him. No Ivy League degree, then a gilt-edged career of corporate law. He would be a hawk on the side of the Right, even if that meant a civil servant's unexciting salary. When Robert Stanfield's life came to an abrupt and dramatic termination in the middle of a federal antitrust hearing, the Stanfield trust also terminated, and it became son Edwin Stanfield's private property.

Despite his affluence, the purposeful, yet colorless, former Attorney General of the minor State of Maryland welcomed protective obscurity in the shadow of Secretary Bowlder, the legal genius who had extricated the nation's threatened power companies from the kind of antitrust action that had fragmented monopolistic Ma Bell into an awkward hydra back in the early eighties. Stanfield had a large iron in a fire that could well consume him were its smoke detected by anyone other than the few select participants. Professional obscurity suited him fine.

The next question from the press, difficult to hear, came from the rear of the briefing room. ". . . Miyamoto, Nippon Newswire." Heads swung, searching out the compact man's pale, round face. "Mr. Secretary, a declaration of war between the United States and any other nation, no matter how small, would have in it the seeds of threat for every nation. Surely, Mr. Secretary, there are other more—shall we say—subtle means of dealing with the serious problem of Mr. Sokolo."

Bowlder shaded his eyes against the flood of light on the dais. "Mr. Miyamoto . . ." He was excellent with names. ". . . I assume you have reference to some manner of covert action?"

"That is so, sir," came the distant response.

"Needless to say, this nation frowns on any such activity directed at another sovereign state."

Well, that was simple and declarative enough, Stanfield mused. The briefing broke up in a flurry of superficial questions, primarily from the TV network people. Then a spate of rudely shouted afterthoughts, following Rylander's pro forma "Thank you, Mr. Secretary," signaled its official end.

Stanfield followed Bowlder out; Rylander several casual steps farther back. Security confined the media crowd to the briefing room. The carpeted corridor was clear and suddenly quiet. The secretary of state preceded his two aides into his big blue-carpeted office and motioned them to the small round conference table near one of the tall windows. The coffee tray was already in place, thanks to Mrs. Julian. She never missed.

"Help yourselves, gentlemen." There was nothing stronger in the room. Bowlder didn't tolerate on-the-job spirits, as he insisted on calling booze of any kind. He would sourly sip an occasional unavoidable sherry at State receptions, or nurse highball glasses of tomato juice at mandatory Washington parties, willing enough that they be assumed bloody Marys.

"Your reading, Davis?"

"Good enough. You weren't in a position to say anything of substance, and you said it well," Rylander blurted. Stanfield envied him the latitude he had to offer top-of-the-head opinions and not worry about career impact. Davis Rylander could go back with ABC News, where he'd come from, or to NBC or CBS, no doubt. At worst, CNN. Talk about nonthreatened. Where, Stanfield wondered, could I go from here? Despite personal wealth, it would be back to Charm City for a dreary federal judgeship at best.

"Winnie?"

Edwin Stanfield detested the nickname, but he hadn't been able to shake it from the day his legal luminary of a father had given it to him. He'd been too young to care then, but it had embarrassed him at Poly, been moth-balled at the U of M, until a Poly classmate had run into him in his sophomore year. After that, it had been too awkward for a grown man to object. He was stuck with the damned thing.

"Mr. Miyamoto had a point," he said cautiously.

"Covert activity?"

"Specifically, the surgical removal of Mr. Sokolo." Stanfield watched Bowlder's tilted-down eyes. Why did men of means so often have downward tilted eyes? There wasn't a blink.

"It would be convenient, wouldn't it?" That was essentially what Bowlder had said before, in the administrative brainstorming session just after the Penn Station bombing. He had then passed it off as no more than wishful thinking, but Stanfield felt he had gotten the message.

It hadn't taken much. When the sickening news of the bombing had filtered through State's myriad offices, he'd sat numb, then had made a flurry of useless phone calls. Nobody up there had known anything. His stomach roiled into acid tension. He hoped against hope that Myra had taken an earlier or later train, or had decided, against her fear of it, to fly.

He could smell his own sweat. Then the call had come, near hysterical, from St. Vincent's emergency. Her right arm had been lacerated, her little finger was missing, her right eardrum shattered, her left ear impaired. He felt a flood of relief. Then concern. Then cold anger. Myra's arm injured, her hand maimed, her hearing probably irrevocably diminished. During the ensuing meeting with Bowlder and the executive level administrative staff, Winnie Stanfield burned to take action, any kind of action, do anything but sit here and listen to the top levels of the U.S. Department of State equivocate.

Then he picked up Bowlder's subliminal signals. They had been signals, hadn't they? "If only I were a free agent . . . If only my hands weren't tied, I'd personally throttle the son of a bitch."

Damned strong words from a cautious man like G. Thomas Bowlder. Such an apparent endorsement had escalated Stanfield's bottled fury into action. And he had the money to buy a lot of it.

Stanfield jerked back to the present, realizing he'd taken too long to acknowledge Bowlder's comment. "Yes, Sokolo's removal would indeed be convenient."

"But, of course, far beyond the purview of the Department."

Stanfield obviously wasn't convinced of that, but he nodded.

"Well, then . . ." Bowlder sighed. "Just where do we go from here? The White House will be asking that very question within the hour. We need some original thinking here."

He chuckled softly. "Davis, didn't I hear you suggest the other day that we could solve our court docket backlogs by requiring the Japanese to take an American lawyer for every car they sell in the U.S.? Any brainstorms on how to salvage this particular situation?"

Didn't Bowlder realize how out of place humor was in this tense discussion? Or did the man need a joke the way most men under tension needed a drink?

Davis Rylander offered a weak smile. Surely neither he nor Bowlder suspected that all of this—today's press briefing and now this postbriefing discussion—was empty rhetoric now. Only one man at State in addition to himself, Stanfield fervently hoped, knew that. That one man was the subordinate Stanfield fully trusted: Dudley Griffin, his own self-effacing aide. Griffin, who looked far older with his white-fringed bald pate than his fifty-one years, was one of the very few tall men with whom Stanfield had ever felt at ease. Griffin was scrupulously aware of the conversational refinement of sitting down quickly with Stanfield, and he invariably maintained a comfortable distance when they necessarily talked on their feet.

Griffin was a former historian with several barely readable, except for the significant one, college texts

74

still in print, and with the recently acquired practical ambition of a dedicated civil servant to get ahead by pleasing his superior. He seemed to enjoy the opportunity to alter a modicum of history through a daring act in which he would have to take no physical risk. And, Stanfield had reflected several times already, if the lid threatened to fly off, the divorced, childless Griffin was . . . expendable. That would sever the linkage.

They had decided that Griffin would use the cover name, "Mr. Johnson."

"And for Christ sake, Griff, use discretion," Stanfield had urged. "For your own sake as well as State's." There seemed a need to imply that the Department was behind this. The man's intense aquamarine stare had told Stanfield that in their initial discussion of the project. Then Griffin himself had come up with the name "Swift Sword."

"Winnie?" Bowlder's Brahmin inflection cut through. "I hope your woolgathering is beneficial to the subject at hand." The man could even scold with grace.

"I was wondering what would have been the course of recent world history had someone had the foresight to eliminate our friend Castro when he was still skulking through the Camaguey hills."

"Classic college ethics class question," Rylander threw in. "If you had a pistol, found yourself in Munich in nineteen thirty-five and knew you would get away with it, would you have shot Hitler in the beer hall?"

"Two cheers for infallible hindsight." Bowlder poured himself a precise second half-cup from the insulated silver pitcher. He took it black. Jamaican Blue Mountain, seventeen bucks a pound, which he scrupulously paid himself. "Knowing what we do at this juncture, we would undoubtedly have trained our theoretical pistol on Stalin and Kaddafi as well. Perhaps even on Marcos and Papa Doc Duvalier."

More corroboration. Wasn't it? When you are receptive, Stanfield realized, the air vibrates with messages. If he'd had any doubts at all, though it was already too late for doubts, they dissolved now. He felt as if a pervasive stiffness had just faded to leave him supple and relaxed.

"Gentlemen," Bowlder announced, setting down his cup and standing, "I thank you for reinforcing the inevitable decision. 'Mr. President,' I shall tell him, 'we have discussed the matter at length, and we are unanimously in accord with whatever course you deem necessary.' That should place it squarely in his hands, thank the good Lord."

Back in his own less sumptuous, but no less comfortable, office, Winnie Stanfield experienced a sudden wave of depression. Marguerite had planned to come to Washington again next weekend as she had two weekends ago. That had been exciting as hell, meeting her at Baltimore-Washington International; she with her famous "American Classic" look altered with a buckwheat honey wig and garish dark glasses, he nervously wearing an old pair of hornrims and a battered brown tam. Probably made him more obvious than if he'd gone up there just as he was, but nobody had recognized either of them.

In his rented Buick, he'd driven them across the Bay Bridge to an Eastern Shore inn. She had been impetuously hungry at dinner and nearly insatiable in the big double bed, as if she'd left all inhibition behind in uptight Manhattan.

The room service whiskey sours were hardly necessary, but he welcomed the playfulness they inspired. God knew, he needed this after a nightmare week with Myra, her maimed hand still tightly bandaged, and her

76

need for him to repeat so many words. He'd needed this, all right.

Marguerite dropped her swizzle stick with its little mallard head into her purse, a souvenir of a glorious night to be. She played a little trick of breaking into irrelevant conversation just as he was about to climax, a device to prolong their intimacy that drove him nuts with escalating urgency. He'd babbled along with her about anything, anything to keep himself from blasting off before she wanted him to. Then she would wind him even tighter.

She asked him about Myra. He opened up about that, all right, and felt a lot better. He told her she would have made a hell of a spy; but he knew she was riskless, so he didn't care what he said there in the rural Maryland darkness. Some technique she had! Then explosive release locked them fiercely together, and when he finally let her go, he was no longer sure what he'd told her. Talk about off-guard!

The more he'd thought about that later, the more potentially disastrous it had loomed. When Griffin had relayed Hammermill's insistence on the names of anyone else who might have the merest inkling of Swift Sword, Stanfield's nagging worry had bubbled into haunting concern.

"No one, Griff. No one at all . . . except possibly—"

"Except possibly whom, Winnie?"

Surely Hammermill would realize she wasn't much of a threat. No threat at all. "Marguerite Falconer," he heard himself say in a voice so low Griffin had strained to hear him.

"The movie actress? My God, Winnie, I didn't even know you knew her. What precisely did you tell her?"

"I don't recall exactly. We were—" He cleared a sudden hoarseness in his throat. "We were at the Blue Mallard Inn on the Eastern Shore last week."

"I get the picture," Griffin said hastily. "You'd had a few, of course."

Stanfield nodded. He wasn't sure he liked this interrogation by his abruptly imperious aide, but getting the nagging worry off his chest did have a salutary effect.

"How about her? She'd had her share, too?"

"We both were pleasantly squiffed, Griff. I doubt she remembers any more details than do I."

"But you do recall mentioning Swift Sword?"

"I may have. It was stupid of me, of course, but I'd say there's a ninety-nine percent chance that nothing registered. I sure as hell don't remember anything she said to me. All I remember is—" He was about to say something extremely personal, but caught himself. "—is that we made a hell of a night of it," he amended. Then he tried to bolster that. "The physical part is all I recall."

"But you also recall mentioning Swift Sword."

Damn! Now he detested this aggressive and persistent questioning by his subordinate, but he had begun to realize that Griffin, through what had been intended as a messenger role, now had something of a hold on him. He bit back a rebuke.

"I may have mentioned it in a moment of—" He attempted a weak grin. "A moment of extreme unction. But possibly not at all." That was a lie. When she had asked about Myra, he had let slip something about the project, realized it was the wine and his need to talk, and stopped. Hadn't he?

When Stanfield had heard the initial and sketchy TV report of Marguerite's accidental death, he'd failed to make any connection. But this morning's Kinchlo

78

column in the *Washington Post* had refocused his thinking. He knew damned well she hadn't a kinky impulse in her lush little body. What she craved, she wanted straight, and a lot of it. With more men than himself, he knew, but straight. Maybe she had been a borderline nympho, but this business about a rope and handcuffs was insane, far out of context with her impish interruption technique to extend their dreamy couplings, then her contented nuzzlings afterward. No accident, Kinchlo. Not that way. Something else had happened up there in New York.

The chill hit him like an injection of ice water. It broke across his shoulders and shot down his spine. Stanfield to Griffin to Hammermill to God-only-knew what kind of creeps worked for Hammermill. Swift Sword had claimed an unintended victim.

Stanfield walked to his office window and stared down into C Street, barely aware of the gridlocked morning traffic. The bastards had not only killed her; they'd desecrated that wonderful little body.

He thought he was going to be sick. Then he began the inevitable bureaucratic rationalization. They all used it: government, civil rights activists, terrorists. In a war you have casualties. His own daughter had been maimed in the action prompted by a warped dictator an ocean away. She was Sokolo's victim.

Marguerite was Swift Sword's victim. He had loved her in a way. That hadn't been difficult. Since Elaine's brief struggle with cirrhosis had left him a widower seven years ago, he had casually loved several diverting women. Marguerite Falconer had been the most imaginative, yet the least complicated. That was why he felt so free with her, so open. Unguarded.

Under Secretary of State Winnie Stanfield reached for the sheaf of papers that choked his in-box, and he tilted back in his soft leather-upholstered chair. In a war, he told himself again, you do inevitably have casualties.

Better Marguerite than himself.

7

DAN PUT IN THE CALL to the *Los Angeles Examiner* at one
P.M.—mid-morning on the West Coast—but he didn't
track Roger Kinchlo down until close to 1:30. The paper's
receptionist referred him to the newsroom. The city
editor, whom Dan hadn't asked for, said Kinchlo hadn't
come in yet, but did give Dan his home number. There,
Dan got Mrs. Kinchlo, who wanted him to call Kinchlo
much later at the paper. After pleading that this was a
professional matter, not a fan or crank call, Dan was
given the number where Roger Kinchlo habitually had
breakfast. "I'm an orange juice, coffee, and toast cook,"
Mrs. Kinchlo confessed. "I don't do Belgian waffles."

At last, the man himself growled out a reluctant
"Yeah?" over a background of dish clatter and voice
gabble.

"Dan Forrest, *NewsLeak*, Mr. Kinchlo. Appreciate
your coming to the phone."

"I don't mind coming to the phone for *Newsweek*."
The grizzly-gruff voice had brightened.

81

Should he let it ride, Dan wondered? Not with what he had in mind. "*News*Leak, Mr. Kinchlo. We're a New York-based national tabloid."

"Shit," said Roger Kinchlo. "So?"

"Your column this morning. You've got a lot of detail in there about the Falconer thing."

"Uh-huh."

"Not all the detail, but a lot. I'm interested in where you got it. The lid's on pretty damn tight here in New York."

"What do you mean, not all the detail?"

Gotcha, Kinchlo! "There was more than you had. The lipstick, for instance." That should set the hook.

"What about lipstick? Uh, what did you say your name was?"

"Dan Forrest. I'm *NewsLeak*'s crime writer."

"What about the lipstick, Dan?"

"What about your source, Roger?"

"You trying for some kind of blackmail here?"

"Come on, Kinchlo. I'm talking trade. Your source for my details."

"Dan, you know I can't blow a source. You know that. And how do I know you've got anything worth trading? How do I know, come to think of it, that you're who you say you are?"

"I'm going to hang up, Kinchlo. You call Information for *NewsLeak*'s number and get back to me if you're interested."

"I'm not sure I am."

"She had words written across her chest in lipstick, Kinchlo." Dan gambled and hung up.

He waited just four minutes until the cubicle's dial phone, probably one of Manhattan's last, jangled.

"Kinchlo, Dan. What words? And how the hell do you know about them?"

"I've got an NYPD pipeline. Look, I don't intend to use your source, but it's important to know who it is."

"Why?"

"Because it looks to me that Falconer's accident was a setup."

"You talking murder?"

"I'm talking a woman who had never been known to be anything but straight. Not even a rumble of anything else. Then this happens. It's way out of context."

"That's a supposition, isn't it? You got anything concrete to back it up?"

"I've got a pretty damned concrete lockout of information by the New York police. That's why I wondered how you got what you got, Kinchlo. That's why I need to know your source."

"What about the God damned lipstick you mentioned?"

"Two words were lettered on her chest. One of them was 'rapture.' "

"Uh-*huh!*" Kinchlo hesitated. A long time. Then he said, "I'll give you the city my source is in. Best I can do. What was the other word?"

"All right, Kinchlo. I'm going to trust you. The other word was 'release.' "

"Weird! Okay, boy. The tip came from D.C."

"Washington? Not from New York? Who in Washington?"

"Can't tell you that, Dan. You got any more?"

"Can't tell you that, Roger."

Kinchlo chuckled. "Okay, tell you what. I'm not going to blow a source, but, if I get anything else that's negotiable, I'll give you a call. I got a feeling you have more in your bag than lipstick graffiti, right?"

"Deal." Dan said and hung up. Fat chance of hearing from a guy like that again. Washington . . . Why Washington?

He pulled out his little wirebound notebook and went through his scribblings. By God, she *had* known somebody down there! Edwin Stanfield, Under Secretary of State.

"Now," said Corkie Brion, "all the jackals are skulking."

They were indeed. Roger Kinchlo's column had laid the Falconer story wide open. Cousin Roy had told Dan that NYPD's public info people were sinking under the load.

"Know what gets me, Daniel?" Corkie sat across from him in the battered booth at Oscar's. They both nursed rank coffees.

He didn't care what her problem was. He had his own. She was part of it. Charlie, damn his scheming soul, had saddled him with a goading shadow. If she were a dumb kid intern, he could have better put up with her. But she was smart; he knew that now. And pushy. And she was getting too far onto his turf.

"What gets me," she said, tapping her spoon handle on the table to bring him back, "is that we're sitting here moping over bad coffee, while the rest of the New York press and a lot of visiting hotshots are crawling all over One Police Plaza on a story that you and I once had a lovely, hot exclusive on."

"Couldn't use it."

"Your promise to Roy? A *NewsLeak* promise is as valid as a real estate promoter's prize offering."

"Maybe that's how you operate. Not me."

"Your *New York Times* background, I suppose. Come on, Daniel, let's get our butts in gear and turn

84

out some copy on this thing! We haven't written a damned word . . . Hey!" He was conscious of her pudgy fingers snapping in his face. "I'm talking to you, Mr. Murrow."

"He was a broadcast reporter."

"They have all the fun. What's bothering you, anyway? Our lousy biweekly publication schedule? Come on, we can whip up a feature on this thing that'll curl their eyelashes in West Whiffle."

"There's something wrong."

"There's what?"

"Something out of sync in all this."

"Of course there is! *That's* the story, Daniel. The rope, the handcuffs, the lipstick. S/M stuff used by an American sex goddess. My God, we've got all the ingredients, and you won't turn on the stove!"

He resisted the impulse to strangle her, gripped the table edge with both hands, and jutted his chin. "Listen to me, Cork. She had no history of aberrations. None. Not a hint. Then we have this elaborate ritual thing. Then we have a police cover-up."

"Because of the mayor's son."

"Yeah, bad luck puts him in the same building, and his occasional neighborly visits with her tied him in. So the mayor's office hushes up what could have been a wild story, then a tip from Washington—of all places—breaks it open by way of a California columnist."

"That's the sequence," she agreed, "even if it doesn't inspire a whole lot of rationale."

"Or does it? Try this. No accident. Somebody does her in and rigs it to look like a kinky sex thing."

"Why?"

"A diversion."

She stared at him.

"To cover up the reason she was killed, Cork. To give the media something to gab about in the grandstand, while they miss what's going on down on the playing field."

"You believe that?"

"It's the only scenario I can come up with that makes sense. You want more coffee? No? Well, hang in a minute."

He took his cup to the counter for a refill. When he came back, he said, "You interviewed Falconer's maid yesterday?"

"Once I got through the hounds. She added zilch."

"You have her number? How about giving her a call right now. I want you to ask her one more question."

When Corkie returned from Oscar's grimy phone nook in the rear of the place, she was a changed woman.

"Daniel, you're . . . Well, I'm impressed. Yes, Marguerite Falconer did visit Washington recently. Just a couple of weekends ago. Before the show opened. Went down on Friday; back on Sunday. The maid has no idea why she went or who she saw. She flew. She wouldn't take the train after the Penn Station thing. And she went alone. Isn't that kind of unusual for a nationally—"

"The Penn Station . . . Bingo!" Dan interrupted. "*There's* the Stanfield connection that's been bugging me. His daughter was clobbered in that blast. By damn, the maid says she doesn't know who Falconer saw in Washington. But we just might!"

"We might?"

He left his second cup untouched.

"Where are you going, Daniel?"

"Washington."

She began to slide out of the booth. He put a hand on her shoulder.

"Alone, Corkie."

That turned out to be his only inaccurate statement of the day.

Hammermill, to his growing consternation, found himself in a bind. He'd thought he would have weeks, perhaps as long as several months, to finalize Swift Sword. Suddenly, the project had telescoped to days. It seemed that President Benjamin Sokolo had changed vacation dates.

That information had reached Hammermill through less than direct routing. To initiate it most unintentionally, Sokolo—an imposing ebony giant—had notified his valet, a wiry, gray-wooled old man the Tuskegee-educated Sokolo wryly called "Mr. Bones."

His real name was Kwame M'Tibi. He was a member of a northern Nandian tribe that had been all but eliminated by Sokolo's troopers in the 1985 coup. His wife, then fifty-eight years of age, had been raped by every member of a seven-man flying squad. She had then killed herself by drinking the sap of a lolo tree, a swift and relatively painless means of suicide. On that day, Kwame M'Tibi had vowed to avenge his beloved Kita.

He moved from the smoking ruins of their home to the capital city in the south. His guise of a subservient old man was easy to maintain. He looked closer to seventy than his sixty-two years. He adopted a slightly hunched posture and pleaded with the chief of the palace household staff for work, any kind of work. From his initial assignment as busboy in the immense crystal-chandeliered and gold-leafed Great Hall, he progressed to assistant waiter.

As such, he caught the eye of Sokolo himself on a state occasion four months ago when he had taken his heart in his hands, then had felt his nerve drain from his body into his shoes. Desperate with sickening fear, he whispered in Sokolo's glistening ear, the one decorated with a two-carat blue-white diamond stud, "Mr. President, I implore you, do not eat the Chicken Kiev!"

This muttered message produced a totally unanticipated scene, which grew to fatal proportions.

"The chicken?" Sokolo rumbled. He eyed the tempting plate prepared by his renegade Austrian chef, Gunter Halz. He turned to his astounded aide, a muscular man in the bright green dress uniform of a Nandian colonel of infantry. "Botatu, bring me a dog."

The colonel shoved out of his high-backed chair to hustle from the hall. The rest of Sokolo's retinue and the jammed Great Hall in general fell into confusion as whispers leaped from table to table. No one touched the chicken now. Several who had tried a bite began to turn an apprehensive gray.

Colonel Botatu returned with a blue-clad corporal of the palace marines who held a small yellowish dog under his arm, a cur he had no doubt found wandering the littered service alley behind the palace grounds.

"On the table," Sokolo ordered.

Colonel Botatu looked distressed. "On the table, Mr. President?"

With a swing of his gold-emblazoned white uniform sleeve, Sokolo swept clear the area beyond his plate. A sterling condiment rack crashed to the floor.

"On the table!" Sokolo growled a second time.

The dog, cringing, made muddy paw prints on the snowy cloth. Sokolo shoved his plate forward. The dog sniffed, glanced up at the bemedaled giant who stood glaring down at the plate, and began to gnaw at the golden brown Chicken Kiev. Three minutes later, he convulsed, fell off the table, whimpered once, and died.

The chef was summoned from the kitchen, ashen-faced and trembling. His poor knowledge of Nandian dialect gave way to a torrent of terrified German, which climaxed in a shrieked *"Nein!"* as Sokolo drew his ponderous Smith & Wesson 586 Distinguished Combat .357 Magnum from its mirror-polished black leather holster and shot the chef through the heart. That stunned the guests in the Great Hall, the visiting Angolan delegation, far more than the two tables of Soviet advisers.

That same afternoon, to his amazement, then growing realization of his advantage, Kwame M'Tibi was appointed personal valet to President Benjamin Sokolo.

The poison with which M'Tibi had laced the president's chicken was an extract of the lolo, essentially the same poison his beloved Kita had used to terminate her disgrace. Now he was in an even better position to avenge her. He was from that day ever alert for the opportunity, though his unexpected failure of nerve had warned him that the act of revenge was not as simple a matter as he had first thought.

Thus it was Presidential Valet Mr. Bones who notified the pock-faced Moroccan clerk in the Aeroflot office at the foot of the Avenue of the Revolution that the president had rescheduled his annual vacation for earlier than usual. Something to do with the female astrologer Sokolo regularly consulted. M'Tibi felt that the Aeroflot clerk would like to be apprised of that unusual schedule adjustment. The presidential valet had learned through the palace gossip chain that the clerk was a seller of information. M'Tibi thought he knew to whom.

The point was that the president's habitual vacation retreat, an artificial private beach blasted and bulldozed out of the rockbound Nandian seacoast, was secluded, accessible—and vulnerable. M'Tibi was aware that the Soviets were rapidly becoming disenchanted with President Benjamin Sokolo. Cuba, Afghanistan, Angola, and

Nicaragua had become heavy enough cash drains without Sokolo's squandering of Nandia's ruble infusions on such gross misappropriations as his recently acquired Boeing 747, with its customized living room, dining room, and bedroom interior. It was Sokolo's third and largest personal aerial luxury in which to travel a republic half the size of Poland.

His palace staff associates would have been astounded that Kwame M'Tibi, Mr. Bones, a simple tribesman from the north, had absorbed all this. They were smugly unaware that he had been district administrator under the old regime, the Royal Household of N'Krumo. He had played the game of intricate politics before.

He was right about the pock-faced clerk, a little predator of a man who routinely forwarded information to the Soviets. But M'Tibi was only partially right. The clerk did give his employers available details on Sokolo's movements. But he also sold such intelligence to two other sources of income, both of whom paid him by the item. One was a well-dressed man with bittersweet chocolate skin who posed as a lawyer, but whom the Aeroflot clerk believed was CIA.

The other was an old wreck of a white man who spent much of each day in the New Era Canteen behind a growing stack of saucers, an apparently harmless drunk who had been shambling along capital city side streets for as long as anyone in the new regime could remember. Only the pock-faced clerk knew the sloppy white man paid for certain information.

Reed, his name was. He had come here in the seventies from Oregon, a retired charter airline pilot chasing rumors of gold in the Nandian—then the Krumoan—hills to the east. There was no gold, but there had turned out to be plenty of useful corruption—then and now. Reed played it like a violin. He was a facilitator.

He was also a seller of information to anyone who would pay. By now, the three-piece-suited CIA black had no faith in him. The Russkies had their own sources. That left the crackpot U.S. freelance outfit that turned out that monthly crap pile of print, *Red Alert*. Came out of Washington and looked official, but it didn't fool Reed when an occasional copy made it to him past the lackadaisical Nandian postal screeners.

He figured he knew where some of the stuff in it came from. Guys like him; except his stuff was pretty good. He slipped his preaddressed envelopes to a Polish Aeroflot flight engineer who mailed them in Rome where the mail was uncensored. The Pole thought they were letters to Reed's nonexistent brother in the U.S. In fact, Reed did address his envelopes to "A.G. Reed," care of J.B. Hammermill's Washington area P.O. box number. The payment, in U.S. cash, came by essentially the same route in reverse. The Polish engineer assumed Reed's brother was sending him conscience money.

In such a convoluted manner did the reset schedule of President Sokolo's vacation reach Hammermill: Kwame M'Tibi to the pock-faced Aeroflot clerk to Reed the drunk to the Polish flight engineer to Italy's postal service to *Red Alert*'s P.O. box. Hammermill needed the information because he knew from the contents of previous battered white envelopes with their Italian stamps that Benjamin Sokolo customarily vacationed in an isolated villa near the town of Agadou on Nandia's Atlantic Coast. The villa was accessible by sea. That was important to the plan he was formulating with Woodman. Crucial was the timing.

In Langley, Virginia, the slender bookish man on the CIA's West African Desk filed the report from the company's Nandian agent on the floppy disc that con-

91

tained all such reports on President Sokolo's behavior characteristics and personal activities.

At the Moscow KGB office in the rear of Lubyanka Prison, a baggy-suited clerk did essentially the same thing with the dispatch that had come in from the KGB man who posed as assistant manager of the Nandian Aeroflot office. The clerk in Moscow would have envied his CIA counterpart, because KGB at Lubyanka had no floppy disc storage capability; the department still laboriously keypunched its data on an endless supply of tan cards.

In the Wheaton office of *Red Alert,* the man known as J.B. Hammermill used the most basic data storage system of all. It was a green metal box of three-by-five ruled white file cards he kept locked in the bottom right-hand drawer of his surplus steel desk. This wasn't going to be so easy, not with this short a notice. How many men? The tighter the team, the better the security. Or should he leave the recruiting and the weapons to Woodman and concern himself only with the financing and the security details? Might be a lot cleaner that way.

He began to finger through the cards for Woodman's number, which he made a point of not remembering.

Charlie Lovett threw his hands high in the air, his characteristic gesture of utter bewilderment.

"Cripes! I never understand the people working for me. And hardly anybody else. Here Kinchlo's column blows the whole Falconer thing wide open, so do you want to hustle your butt over to Police Plaza PI? Hell, no! You want to waltz off to Washington. Washington! I thought you were hooked on a scandal, Dan."

"Corkie's our scandal mainliner, Charlie."

His suddenly roseate face a striking contrast to his awry white crest, Charlie swung from Dan to Corkie Brion. "Well?"

"What can we do with our lousy publication schedule that won't already have been done by the competition by the time we go to press? I checked. Police Plaza is up to its holsters in media."

Nice, Cork, Dan thought. We'll go down together. "Right," he said. She was. "Charlie, they're surface scratchers, hung up on the sex details. I'm after more."

"*We're* after more," Corkie reminded them.

"We're [okay, Cork?] after what's . . . what's behind this thing. The, hell, the anatomy—"

"*The Anatomy of a Scandal.*" Charlie held his hands out in a movie director framing gesture. "I can see it now. Up in lights. Come on, Dan, we're a damned tabloid, not the Screen Writers' Guild."

Dan shrugged at Corkie. "All I asked him for was a few bucks to go to Washington."

"And car rental and the corporate Amex card," Charlie stormed. "That's damned near cart blank."

"Let me lay it out for you one more time," Dan offered patiently. "First, Falconer is done in—"

"You'll have to prove that."

"I'm trying to prove that! Just take it as a given for a minute, will you, Charlie?"

"I heard it all already. So you think there's a D.C. connection."

"That I do. She's been linked with a pretty big name down there, and not long before the rope trick, she snuck out of town in that direction. So says the maid."

"That's enough to build a story on?"

"That's enough to look into, Charlie, while the rest of the pack is baying away up here."

"Nyuh-huh." Charlie massaged his facial sags. "You'll rent from Budget?"

"From Budget. A Chevette, if I have to."

"You have to. No downtown hotel, damn it."

"For *NewsLeak,* I'm always a fringe area man."

"No fancy fillay minions."

"Ronald McDonald and I have a gastric love affair."

Charlie sighed. "Oh, crap."

"I take it that's today's code for affirmative?"

"Unh—"

"I'm going, too, of course," Corkie cut in, instantly screwing up the nicely developing investigative junket.

"Hell with that," Charlie rumbled. "Tagging along in New York is one thing—"

"Tagging along! Who interviewed Rinaldo Patton? Who got Holley Junior to admit he was japing Falconer off and on?"

"Japing?" Charlie flicked meringue eyebrows at Dan.

"And who," Corkie barged on, "was told she was in on this thing fifty-fifty?"

Charlie shook his ponderous head. "It's the budget, kid. Not personal."

"I've got a week coming," she ranted. "I'll go on my own time. The car won't cost any more for two. I'll buy my own Big Macs. Pay for my own cheapo motel room—"

"Oh, hell," Charlie surrendered. "Save your damned receipts. Get her out of my space, Dan. *But don't come back without a story, the two of you!"*

On Sunday, of all days, after five traffic-infested rain-slick interstate hours, they were residents of a concrete-slabbed salesmen's stopover near Largo along the eastern sweep of the Capital Beltway. The Barren Hilton, she tagged it. Cement hallways with skimpy maroon runners; soda and ice machines on odd floors only. The elevator trembled as if it were afraid of heights. They drew third-floor rooms with a connecting door. That was the desk clerk's automatic assignment. Corkie was the one who made the discovery that their common door's lock was broken.

"Hell with it," Dan said wearily. "You're safe with me, kid."

"I'm safe with everybody. You ever married, Daniel?" They sat at a red-topped table in a corner of the motel's plain pine Snak Shoppe; she with an immense bowl of glutinous chili and a cheeseburger that looked as if it had been ironed; he with Swiss on white. When he upended the mustard squeeze bottle, yellow water squirted out first.

"Daniel?"

He realized he'd been a prime pain in the ass all the way down in the bouncy little tan Chevette, p.o.'d because she had been smart enough to wangle this trip out of Charlie, when she was no more needed down here than wings on a woodchuck.

"Once," he growled. "I was married once."

"What happened?"

"She didn't know about Alanon. I drank her right out of the house. Them was the days. Don't push it, Cork."

"Sorry." She sounded as if she was. "About to-morrow . . ."

"What about tomorrow?"

"When you go to the State Department, I'm going with you."

"That a question or a demand?"

"All right, can I?"

"What good can you do?"

"I can watch who you interview, Daniel. Who are you going to interview?"

"Couldn't get to Stanfield Friday. The appoint-ment's with some guy named Rylander, their Chief of

Public Information. Nobody says PR anymore. What do you mean, watch?"

"Body language. I used to work for a fund-raising outfit. Melton Jannis Company. We went out in teams to call on potential big givers to the churches that hired us. One to make the pitch, the other to watch. I was a watcher." She dipped into the viscous chili.

"What kind of body language?" She was lumpish and mouthy, but he was finding her a source of continuous surprises.

"Slumping is a drop dead message. Arms folded, a defense. Leaning forward means interested. Best of all is dilated pupils."

"What's that mean?"

"Excitement. Thinking hard. You got to him."

"You actually watched for that kind of stuff?"

"You kidding? Altogether, I helped raise three million dollars."

He paid the whole check, waving away her offer to split it. "Forget it. Cheaper than if we'd had real food."

Upstairs, after he'd showered and was pulling on his pjs, he heard her thump on the connecting door. "G'night, Daniel. Don't worry about the busted lock. I don't sin in my sleep."

"Simmer down, Cork. We're going to hit State at nine sharp. If you aren't ready to leave here by eight-fifteen, you're on your own."

But he was the laggard stunned to be jolted awake first by the smell of coffee, then by the imposing sight of her in a voluminous royal blue sack, banging a tray through their common door. "Brought it up for us from Roach Haven."

He felt scruffy, defenseless, and contrite. "You're a little hard to figure."

He'd brought no robe. She threw him his raincoat, then cleared the rickety table near the single window. When he came out of the bathroom, they ate overlooking the parking area. The toast was limp, but the coffee was a modicum better than the stuff at Oscar's.

"Suppose I'd asked you to chase down for this?" He gestured toward the cluttered table with his coffee cup.

"I'd have told you I don't do windows, either."

"Yeah, you would have."

She plucked at the roll of skirt across her middle. "Inside this damned cocoon I know there's a butterfly, Daniel. But—" Her voice stalled out. She looked away. "Oh, go shave your face."

8

DUDLEY GRIFFIN had lied. When the tabloid reporter called to set up an interview with Stanfield, Griffin had informed the man that the under secretary was unavailable. Well, not a lie; a before-the-fact fact. When he'd told Stanfield the name of the paper, the under secretary instantly became unavailable.

And he asked Griffin, "Why me? Why not Bowlder? Wouldn't a paper like that revel in an exclusive interview with the secretary of state himself?" He pondered a moment. "Call the man back. Send him to Rylander. That's logical enough. But I want you to be in on it to give me a reading."

Griffin smiled his tight little smile. "I've already set it up that way."

All he got for that was Stanfield's perfunctory nod. Such, Griffin reflected ruefully, was the bureaucratic reward for initiative. "Why?" Stanfield asked again, half to himself this time. "Why would that crappy little rag want to interview me?"

Why, indeed, Griffin wondered now, as he waited in his small office adjoining Stanfield's significantly larger and much higher-budgeted square footage. A New York-based national muckracking tabloid . . .

He felt an ominous tightening of the chest and a loosening below the belt. New York. For the first time since he'd begun the diverting game of covert liaison for Stanfield, Dudley Griffin began to wonder whether he had made a serious error in departing the reassuring tranquility of Nassau's ivied walls.

The phone jangled at 9:05. "Come on down, Griff." Rylander's gritty voice. "They're here."

The four of them sat around the small conference table in Rylander's office. The State Department's Chief PIO decorated as he dressed: Midwestern Rotary. Inelegantly framed eight-by-ten glossies hodgepodged the walls: Rylander shaking hands, eating barbecue, sailing, jogging with an array of recognizables from all three Kennedys, right through lots of Lyndon's and Jimmy's people, but only a few of Reagan's. Rylander professed political agnosticism, but the photos denied his denials.

Griffin was aware that his greeting had been perfunctory, but not only had he been put off by the New York aspect and the grubby little paper that had wormed its way in here, he also had been rebuffed by the looks of both these people. He had anticipated Rylander's informal tweeds, but the middle-aged reporter's raincoat was a disgrace, his brown plaid sports coat was more appropriate to nearby Laurel Raceway, and the man's shoes needed immediate attention.

That was inappropriate enough for a call on the U.S. Department of State, but the woman! A walking tent.

When they'd all gathered around Rylander's mahogany table, Griffin had primly hiked up his knife-

99

creased navy blues and sat stiffly. Somebody had to maintain departmental decorum. Rylander, of course, stoked the pipe that Bowlder permitted him only in his own office, and promptly filled the place with stifling haze.

"Mr. Forrest, Miz Brion, what can we do for you this morning?"

Forrest, Griffin quickly assessed, was far from a Pulitzer candidate. He had a downwardly mobile aura: in his forties; quick brown eyes, but set in tired sockets; pale, thinning hair; slightly off-center nose. Maybe a barroom brawler once, now showing a touch of middle-aged spread.

The woman had let it all go. Early thirties with the heft of a forty-year-old who didn't give a damn. No Woodward and Bernstein, these two. If Rylander hadn't had a slow day, they wouldn't have made it in here at all.

"We did want to talk directly with Under Secretary Stanfield," Forrest said.

Rylander took out his broiling pipe. "I'm sure that Mr. Griffin here explained the under secretary's busy schedule. You can imagine the impact of the Sokolo situation on our availabilities. I'm afraid Mr. Griffin and I are the best the department can offer at this point in time. Just what was it you wanted to see Secretary Stanfield about?"

"It's something of a personal matter."

Deep in his gut, Griffin felt an early warning twinge.

Rylander packed down the pipe's loosening coals with the flat of a worn nickel-plated lighter. "What else for a publication that calls itself *NewsLeak*? What's your particular department there, Mr. Forrest?"

"Crime."

Griffin's rectal muscles tightened involuntarily.

100

"Crime?" Rylander chuckled. It struck Griffin that the press chief was toying with these people. "And you, Miz Brion?"

"Celebrity gossip." Obviously a woman with no evident pretentions.

"Crime and gossip." Rylander chuckled again. Griffin's alarm system didn't relent. Get them out of here, Davis. Get them out of here.

"Come now, Forrest. Crime and gossip in the State Department? Well, gossip, sure. What organization doesn't have an ample supply of that? None of it more than in-house interest." Rylander smiled benignly. "Don't tell me you two have come two hundred fifty miles on nothing more than a fishing expedition?"

Forrest leaned forward and flattened his palms on the tabletop, an aggressive gesture. But if he thought he was going to shake up unflappable Davis Rylander, he was off on the wrong byroad. "No, Mr. Rylander, we came two hundred fifty miles to ask Mr. Stanfield where he was two weekends ago."

Rylander's pipe stopped halfway to his mouth. "That sounds like a police question. And a personal one. What kind of interview is this?"

Griffin sat frozen, arms tightly folded. Let Rylander carry this, all of it. The reporter's single query had been a corker, but Rylander, in his innocence, was methodically drowning it in Dutch Uncleism. So far, so fine.

But something wasn't right here. Griffin could feel that in the smoke-laden, increasingly tense air. Something . . . the damned woman. She should be hanging on Rylander's words, but she wasn't. Her disturbingly alert brown agate eyes were riveted on his own.

He tried not to show a sign of noticing that, of being disturbed by that. What the hell was with her?

Forrest shrugged. "We heard he knew Marguerite Falconer."

"The actress?"

"We heard she disappeared that particular weekend. We—"

"Now just hold it!" Rylander's voice had an abrupt edge Griffin hadn't heard before. "If you want to talk State Department business, the Penn Station tragedy, the Sokolo response, our response to the Sokolo response, okay. That's legitimate material. But if you're here on some sort of personal smear of Under Secretary Stanfield—or anybody else in this department—then you are on the wrong wavelength, my friend. Unless you have something more constructive to offer than we've heard so far, this so-called interview is terminated."

They left in disarray, Griffin was pleased to note. He had a new respect for Davis Rylander. Hidden in those rumply tweeds, the man had something wholly unexpected. A steel spine.

"Beautifully managed," Griffin commented. "I will pass that on to the under secretary."

"Now you know how to handle reporters from that particular variety of paper. Short shrift." Davis Rylander looked pleased with himself. At his office door, he even gave Griffin a friendly shoulder pat. "Short shrift," he repeated. "They're the acne on the face of the profession."

That I won't pass on, Griffin thought.

On Virginia Avenue, the wind cut through Dan's raincoat as if it were cheesecloth. The parking garage was two frigid blocks northwest.

"So give me a reading, Cork. What could you make of Rylander's body clues?"

"I didn't watch him."

"You didn't watch him! What was the point of your going—"

"I watched Griffin." She matched him stride for stride, a hiker imposing enough to scatter oncoming foot traffic.

"Why him?"

"Why was he there? He didn't contribute anything."

"Ah-ha! To watch *us*. You watched the watcher. Not bad."

She flipped up the collar of her coat. "God, it's cold! I thought we were in the South."

He ransomed the Chevette and turned its heater on full. Her lips lost their bluish tint at they passed between the Ellipse south of the White House and the Washington Monument grounds on Constitution. She didn't use lipstick.

"Where are we going, Daniel?"

"East."

"East?"

"I don't have any idea where we're going," he admitted. "We didn't get anywhere at all this morning, and that was my best shot. Hell, it was my only shot."

When they were held up by traffic near the Museum of Natural History, she said, "We ought to hit on Griffin. He was stretched tighter than a tennis net. Clamped arms, sunk way back in his chair, the whole defense bit. And when you mentioned Falconer, his pupils went off like railroad crossing signals. He didn't want to hear that name, Daniel."

He turned to her. "You sure about that?"

"Would I lie?"

Abruptly, Dan swung north into Twelfth Street, passed IRS and the Federal Triangle, turned west on K, then north again on Fifteenth.

"I don't know where we are," Corkie said, "but you've been here before."

"In a past life. Ah, there it is."

"*The Washington Post* Building?"

"You just gave this thing some focus, Cork. Look for a parking garage."

They found one an acceptable walk distant, stashed the Chevette, and went through the ubiquitous Washington security sign-in paranoia a few minutes after ten. Only at the desk of the paper's library, nee morgue, were they questioned. Newspaper morgues once were open to all comers. Now many of them were open only to staff.

"Ben said it would be okay." Dan wore a perplexed country boy frown.

"Mr. Bradlee?" The gray lady shrugged. "Well, sure . . ."

"I'll take Stanfield," Dan told Corkie. "You take Griffin."

The job took until noon. Eyes bleary from the glare of a torrent of microfilmed readouts, they got out of there as casually as they had gotten in, each with a dandy set of scrawled notes.

"Hey, screw Charlie," Dan announced back on the chilly sidewalk. "The Mayflower is just a couple blocks west."

In the grill's dark-paneled seclusion, they culled their jottings for significance—an elusive game, Dan realized, when you aren't at all sure precisely what you are looking for.

"Federal departments are all set up along the same lines. The secretaries are political appointees. Like Bowlder. They come and go on political winds. They bring in their own next level people—the Stanfields. Next plateau down is the one that really keeps the

104

bureaucratic wheels turning—the career civil servants. Griffin's level."

"Except he isn't one of those third level fixtures, Daniel. He's out of Princeton just a year ago. He testified before the Pinelas Commission, which was how Stanfield apparently met him. That was . . ." She flipped through her little ring-bound notebook. "A little over a year ago."

"Ties in. The *Post*'s Stanfield file had a good bit on that. Senator Pinelas was wonked out over covert actions against friendly governments. Put a new chill on the CIA, almost a replay of what happened to it in the seventies."

Corkie had tied into her steak sandwich, while he culled his notes. She straightened abruptly. "One of Griffin's books was— Wait a minute." She wiped her fingers on the beige linen napkin and pawed back into her notebook. "Here it is. *Overthrow: The Coup d'Etat in the 20th Century.*"

"Wonder which side he was on?"

"According to the clip, he claimed that covertly tossing out despots isn't all that bad. That was the gist of his testimony before the commission."

"Interesting. Stanfield testified the same way. That is where he met Griffin, and he hired him a couple weeks later, so the *Post* reported." Dan riffled his pages of notes. "Yeah, got it right here. You're right. Griffin's an academia nut, not a career bureaucrat. And Stanfield's a— Wait a minute." He flipped back a few pages. "He's a crusader type. Former attorney general of Maryland. Put away half a dozen key people hooked up with that state's casualty insurance swindles, including two state senators."

"Tough cookie."

105

"You don't make it in Maryland politics by being a swell guy, Cork." He took a hefty bite of his crab cake, and checked his notes while he chewed. "Here it is. He's on record supporting direct U.S. intervention in Nicaragua, heavy weapons for Savimbi in Angola, establishment of an antigovernment force in Libya."

"A real fire breather."

"Seems so, when you put it all together. I pulled this stuff out of a lot of different stories."

"All true-blue right-thinking American motivations. You really can't totally condemn any of it."

"You can see that negotiation doesn't seem to be a Stanfield strong point. Pair that with Professor Dudley Griffin's text romancing violent overthrow, and you have a matched set."

"You know something, Daniel? We've invested the whole morning in these two guys, filled two notebooks with them, yet we don't have one blessed fact to tie Stanfield in with the death of Marguerite Falconer, except that he knew her."

"And the fact that the tip to Kinchlo that opened up the voodoo sex aspects of her death came from Washington. And Stanfield possibly saw her not too many days before she died."

"Prove that."

"You got me, Cork."

"See where we are? Nowhere."

He finished the crab cake in glum silence. Then he brightened. "I just thought of a straw to clutch."

"We're that desperate?"

"We're close. Wait right here."

"Where else? You've got the credit card."

A handful of change got him through to Cousin Roy, who routinely brown-bagged it at his desk when he wasn't on the street.

"I take it the case isn't so closed now, Roy, thanks to Kinchlo?"

"Officially, it's still accidental death. Unofficially, well . . ."

"You made an inventory list when you went over her apartment, right?"

"SOP, Dan."

"Got it there? See if you can find anything that points to a weekend in the Washington area earlier this month. Credit card slip, hotel bill maybe."

He heard paper rustle, heard Roy cough, heard typewriters and voices. Heard nothing for a while.

"Not a damned— Wait a minute. Maybe this. 'Swizzle stick, plastic, blue with duck head, imprinted *Blue Mallard Inn, Easton, Maryland.*' What do you think, Cousin?"

"I think you're a hell of a cop, Roy."

He hung up, elated. Then the boost began to fade. "Could be something or nothing," he told Corkie back at their table. "Maybe she'd carried the thing around for years, like a lucky charm."

"Why don't I go up to that place?"

"To see if some desk clerk remembers two people from two weeks ago?"

"I'll scrounge up their pictures. She ought to be easy enough to find in almost any paper at the moment. Or in *People* magazine."

"And Stanfield?"

"*Post* files again. I could get a print-out."

"If they went there for a quiet weekend, Cork, I'm sure she wore a wig or something, and he no doubt had shades or whatever. He's not one of the best-known faces around, anyway. And you don't for a second think they registered in his name? Certainly not in hers. You'd just be wasting time and mileage."

He picked up the check. "You think Griffin is a bundle of repression, so we're going to do something with that. We didn't get anywhere on his turf. Let's see how he reacts to ours."

Griffin didn't like this, didn't like it at all. He wanted to be on his way to his upper Connecticut Avenue apartment, not worming through East Capital Street traffic to some damned Largo motel.

But that tired-looking reporter had been adamant on the phone. "Sorry, but we're tied up here. You'll have to come to us."

Griffin was about to tell— What was his name? Forrest? He was about to tell him that an interview was impossible tonight, or any other time, until the man said, "It concerns Under Secretary Stanfield and Marguerite Falconer, Mr. Griffin. New evidence. And we have a good indication that you are involved, sir. We want to give you the chance to talk with us in confidence with no witnesses around. Otherwise . . ." He'd left that hanging. An eloquent threat.

Good God Almighty! Now Dudley Griffin drove in the opposite direction from his familiar route home. He hoped Juneau, his Samoyed bitch, would hold out until he got back to the apartment to walk her.

East Washington's low-income blocks were shrouded in gloomy half-light, though the time was not yet 6:00 P.M. A brooding overcast had begun to reflect the glow of the downtown he had just left. As he crossed the bridge over the Anacostia River and Kenilworth Avenue, the evening seemed to close in. The street became Maryland Route 214, and he drove through ill-planned suburbs and commercial strips, the inevitable dross of a metro area that was growing too fast. A light rain, more of a dismally thick mist, began to filter out of the op-

108

pressive overcast. Griffin fervently hoped it would not freeze. Washington traffic was pure hell on icy streets.

Six miles beyond the Anacostia Bridge, the metallic green Pontiac crossed beneath the Capital Beltway near Largo's loose sprawl. Two minutes after that, Griffin pulled into the motel's poorly lighted parking lot and made certain he locked all four doors.

He walked head-down through the drizzle, the Pakistani-style hat he affected in cold weather alternately saffron, then sickly green in the neon flares of the animated entrance sign. Sic transit gloria. Swift Sword had begun in a flash of Stanfield's inspired anger. Griffin had been acutely aware of the man's impatience with the power of "crackpotheads of stagnant states," as Stanfield termed them, and of Stanfield's abhorrence of their power to "jerk the U.S. around, because we're too damned world class to do anything definitive about it." He'd watched Stanfield's frustration mount from Khomeini to Kaddafi; then Sokolo and his Penn Station bomb and a bloodied daughter brought Stanfield's preoccupation with theory to the hard cutting edge they'd named Swift Sword.

Heady stuff for a middle-aged history professor. Griffin couldn't sleep for the early excitement of it. Now he was again becoming unable to sleep for further reasons. They hit him like sudden sweats. What they were doing was monstrously illegal, but in the new politics of terrorism, it could prove to be morally right. "It *is* morally right, Griff. Let me worry about the nuances."

Easy for you to have said, sir. You weren't to be the point man, now walking across this dreary parking lot in a nondescript Maryland suburb of D.C. because an over-the-hill reporter from a crackpothead tabloid seems to be threatening a touch of blackmail.

Griffin spotted a wall placard indicating the direction to the elevator—one of those maroon plastic rectangles with the lettering routed out to expose an underlying white layer. Class all the way. He followed the walkway beneath the second-floor balcony's overhang around a corner to an entrance door at the east end of the ground-floor corridor.

The steel elevator door, its many paint layers randomly chipped, was halfway down the hall, its current top layer an institutional tan. The lobby was visible at the corridor's far end. He hoped the place was as inactive as the scatter of cars in the parking area indicated. He preferred to be seen by as few people as possible in this out-of-context location, though he was far from what the press would term a public figure. Swift Sword had already inspired this much clutching edginess.

Behind one of the room doors near the elevator, a woman giggled, cried a muffled, "Oh, not that again, Arnie!" clearly not meaning it, then giggled anew. Griffin grimaced. It was barely suppertime.

The elevator door slid open in a series of little jerks. The car smelled of the ghost of boozing past. He jabbed the grime-edged plastic "3" button. Thank God he wasn't going any higher. The car shuddered all the way up.

Room 306 was five doors along the hall to the left. He hesitated then tapped discreetly.

"It's open." Through the thin panel, he recognized the world-weary voice of the reporter whom Rylander had waltzed around so adroitly this morning. Maybe this wouldn't be any more difficult. Princeton and the U.S. State Department vs. the supermarket press.

The man sat in shirt-sleeves at a skimpy little table near the window at the far end of the deplorable room. This was the kind of motel room Griffin had seen in old gangster movie reruns. How ludicrously melodramatic!

What made it more so was the sickly glow from the dated Art Deco lamp on the table. The rest of the room was in shadow.

"Take a seat, Mr. Griffin." The only one available was directly across the little table from the reporter. Griffin, in his damp coat, sank into the chair. He placed his hat in his lap. "You mentioned something about—"

"About a connection between Marguerite Falconer and Under Secretary Stanfield. The New York police have found such evidence in her personal effects."

Was the man bluffing? "The under secretary has been photographed on several occasions with Miss Falconer. Fund-raising events, primarily. Public events, Mr. Forrest. There's no news in that anymore." He felt more confident after Forrest's ineffective fishing. Rylander would have been impressed by his parry.

He heard a rustle behind him and whirled.

"Good evening, Mr. Griffin."

Where had Forrest's heavyset partner come from? Hadn't he shut the door when he'd come in? Then Griffin noticed the connecting door, now open. Cozy. Forrest and her? This morning her hard stare had drilled right through him, as warm as a police matron's. Took all kinds.

"Let's not waste each other's time, Mr. Griffin." Forrest sat stiffly, hands folded on the tabletop. "We know Miss Falconer came to this area two weekends ago. She stayed at the Blue Mallard in Easton. We know she's been linked with Stanfield. They were together up there, weren't they?"

Through a swirl of apprehension, Griffin managed to keep his voice cold. "I cannot allow you to link the under secretary's name with the Falconer tragedy."

111

"He's already linked," the woman said from the connecting doorway.

A burst of hot sweat made Griffin's undershirt clammy. They knew about the Blue Mallard. Maybe they *weren't* bluffing!

Forrest placed his hands flat on the tabletop. "We're going to be candid, Mr. Griffin. Everyone we have interviewed who knew Marguerite Falconer well swears she was not into the kind of thing the police say she died from. Nobody has said murder yet, but that's the conclusion we've come to."

Now Griffin strove mightily to control his voice. "Who's come to?"

"Miss Brion and I. Everything we've learned points away from an accident and toward a killing."

"A killing?" Griffin realized he was parroting Forrest's phrases to buy time. How much had these two unlikely reporters learned? How much was chillingly accurate guesswork? His forehead was wet. He had no choice but to pull out a handkerchief. A dead giveaway. At Swift Sword's outset, when it was still an abstract game, he had been confident that he had far better self-control than this.

"He's implicated," the woman said abruptly.

"Who?"

"Your boss, Griffin. Implicated in the death of Marguerite Falconer."

Dudley Griffin felt a sensation much like a thin sheet of cold water sweeping downward from his bald skull to break across his shoulders.

"That," he managed, "is patently ridiculous." But how much did they know? If they had tagged Stanfield, wasn't it inevitable that he, too, would be dragged down in the ensuing debacle? Why in the world had he come here with the arrogance to believe he could face down two tabloid reporters by himself, without Rylander to run a protective screen? Arrant stupidity, and now it was too late to back out.

Or was it? He folded his arms and sat back in the hard chair. "I don't have to tell you a thing."

"Of course not," Forrest agreed, "but there is such a thing as protection of sources. You're aware that reporters are willing to serve jail terms rather than expose a source?"

Griffin could not read the man. One minute, Forrest seemed a last-ditch-job hack; the next, an uncomfortably sharp, well-educated investigator. The woman? He'd been put off early on by her unremitting stare in Rylander's office this morning. She was just as frigidly relentless now. He shouldn't have come here.

"I don't have to talk to you people." He shoved the chair back and jerked to his feet. The hat tumbled to the floor. He bent to retrieve it. "I don't have to stay here."

Forrest's wide face tilted upwards. "That's true enough. But if you leave now, you're no source."

"Damned right. I haven't told you anything."

"So there's no protection."

Griffin, turning toward the door, stopped. "From what?"

Forrest's eyes held his. "From our investigation, Mr. Griffin."

"Investigation of what!" Dudley Griffin snorted. He strode out of the room and slammed the door behind him.

But in the hall, his knees felt like gelatin. He couldn't stop an aggravating trembling of his thigh muscles. His underarms were sticky and his crotch was uncomfortably moist. They knew . . . something. But how much? Enough to implicate him in Swift Sword?

113

He reached his apartment a frightened man, put Juneau on her leash, and walked her around the darkened block in an attempt to settle his nerves. Then he prepared his standard mid-week supper of bean soup, canned corned beef with a poached egg, and a half brick of hastily warmed frozen peas. He nearly let the peas boil dry.

Griffin had just suffered the trauma of realizing he was not a brave man.

His supper was tasteless. He envied the Samoyed in the corner of the kitchen happily gobbling her Dog Chow and beef parts, her only worry the elementary one of wondering when he would arrive home each evening.

He should have stayed at Princeton, but what repressed academician could have rejected the flattering call from the State Department? And what under secretarial aide could resist the opportunity to dabble in a bit of intrigue in behalf of the man who had brought him there? Loyalty—plus the thrill of helping to plot a clandestine international event—had gotten him into this increasingly terrifying bind.

No. He was lying to himself. Loyalty hadn't prompted him to apprise Hammermill of Stanfield's loose-lipped liaison with Marguerite Falconer. The inevitable CYA impulse had done that: cover your ass, Griffin. Some loyalty, that. He had betrayed—was that the correct word? Hell, yes. He'd betrayed Stanfield to Hammermill because he was afraid of what the gossipy mouth of an actress could do to Swift Sword.

Come on, Griffin, it's time for frankness with yourself. You were afraid of what she could do to *you*.

He had three—no, four—choices. None of them was a real way out of the quicksand that Swift Sword was becoming. He could tell Stanfield that the *NewsLeak* people apparently had him linked with Falconer. Or he could tell Hammermill of that dangerous development.

No, by God, he couldn't open up to either one. That would be admitting he'd had further contact with those damned reporters, a tactical error he knew instinctively he should not reveal.

He could do nothing. But if the *NewsLeak* people had what they'd said they had, that would ultimately lead to the implication of one Dudley Griffin.

Or he could go for Forrest's promise of protection.

He rinsed his plate and silver and slid them into the dishwasher. He knew now that there really was no choice at all. The time was at hand for distancing, Professor Griffin. Time to pull out of this suddenly lethal game. It would mean resignation from State, but that was infinitely better than the personal disaster he seemed inevitably headed for at this late moment. Forrest and the big woman knew about Stanfield and Falconer at the Blue Mallard. Now they were pushing hard into that. Had the actress said something significant before she died? Had she perhaps written something about Swift Sword; a note, a letter to a friend?

Stanfield had assured him they'd both been in their cups and intent on only one thing. But who really knew a woman's state of mind at a time like that? Griffin's experience had been limited to one embarrassing affair during a conference years ago. She'd laughed at his awkwardness, and that convinced him he didn't really need women, didn't trust them. He did not truly regret what had happened to Marguerite Falconer. He was far more concerned about Forrest's female partner. She had stared straight into his craven soul.

The Samoyed stood between his knees, her fluffy white wolf's head resting on his thigh. He absently kneaded the rabbit-soft fur behind her ears.

115

He wanted out.

With protection. Had Forrest meant what he'd said about that? The man's paper was one of those checkout counter impulse things, but the man himself was all Griffin had. Him and the hard-eyed woman. Would they leave the little fish alone if he gave them a bigger one?

Better a live coward, he reflected as he looked up the Largo motel's number in the Washington Metro White Pages. He hesitated one last time. Then he dialed.

"Mr. Forrest? Dudley Griffin."

No surprise on the other end. Had Forrest expected this call?

"I'm only the messenger," Griffin blurted. "You've got to leave me out of it."

"We'll do what we can."

"I need more than that, Forrest. Remember what you said about protecting a source?"

"You're not a source yet, Mr. Griffin. You haven't told us anything."

"I can give you some help. A lead. But no more than that." He didn't want to be the direct implement of Swift Sword's exposure. Let Forrest and the woman get the specifics elsewhere, remote from himself. But he could point them in the right direction.

"Hammermill." Griffin licked dry lips. Too late for recall now. "J.B. Hammermill. He publishes one of those nut fringe newsletters called *Red Alert*."

"Locally?"

"In Wheaton."

"What's the connection?"

"I'm afraid that's all I can afford to tell you, Mr. Forrest."

There was a silence. Then Forrest said, "Thank you, Mr. Griffin. If that leads anywhere, consider yourself a protected source."

116

Dudley Griffin nodded at the phone on his kitchen wall and hung up the slippery handset. He wasn't the man for this. He'd gotten himself in far over his head when he had helped put Swift Sword together. Now he had taken the step to start its dismantling before it rolled over him.

9

"WHAT IN HELL are we getting ourselves into?" Dan stared at the phone, as he replaced it on the low set of drawers beside the TV stand.

"Here's *Red Alert.*" Corkie had listened to the conversation with Griffin, sharing the receiver with Dan. She held her place in the phone book with a forefinger. "Rathmussen Tower in Wheaton, like the man said. Where's Wheaton?"

"Maryland suburbs, north of the city. Talk about out of context!"

"I wasn't, but I was thinking it."

"What can a looney newsletter have to do with Marguerite Falconer handcuffed and dead in her Manhattan bathtub?"

"I'm just a country girl, Daniel. From Ohio's tornado alley. Head cheerleader for dear old Clarksburg H.S. in my pre-adipose years. No better than Phi Beta Kappa at OSU. Next, the fund-raising bit, then a job with *Vogue,* until I'd had it up to here with fad. *NewsLeak* appeals to my killer instinct, but I'm still a country girl

118

at heart. Maybe that's why none of this makes sense to me. Does it to you?"

"No. Look up Hammermill, J.B."

"I just did, Daniel. In the D.C. and Maryland suburban books. He must have an unlisted number, or he lives out of the area."

"We'll try to get a line on Hammermill and *Red Alert* tomorrow. What did you make of Griffin's reactions?"

"One scared man. I could feel the fear like an electric charge. We really got him sweating."

"Check. And his phone call tells us he's in something he wants to get out of. Enough to give us a tip." Dan stripped off his tie.

"We're getting undressed?"

"I'm going to bed, Cork. That'll be a step up from sitting around listening to the paint flake."

"Doesn't say much for present company. I'm not at all tired, Daniel." She plunked into one of the chairs that flanked the rickety table by the window. "Why don't you tell me the story of *your* life?"

"You kidding? I'm just a simple country boy. From Ulmer, PA."

"So far, I love it."

Damned if he didn't find himself unloading on her; an edited version because there were things no one needed to know. Not until he'd taken her from the little Pennsylvania coal town to 'Nam, then through Syracuse U's Newhouse School of Public Communications, and the boozy downhill spin from the *Times* into Bellevue, then the virtual parole to *NewsLeak*, did he realize how effective was her don't-really-care interview technique.

Or was it this bare-bones room in this middle drawer motel with a chubby lady? The busted connecting door

119

made it a setup she didn't object to. But with Corkie Brion? Come on, Forrest, pay attention to your work.

"I've got a gnaw, Cork, and when I get a gnaw, it shakes me. This thing is beginning to turn into a six-hundred-pound gorilla. It began as a neat little celebrity death—"

"Not so neat, not so little. More like bizarre."

"I'll give you that. But now we're more than two hundred miles out of home territory, and we're beginning to see our bobber go under at the U.S. Department of State. And out of left field comes somebody named Hammermill on a tip called in by a well-shaken bureaucratic fud trying hard to slip under *our* protective feathers. All that is what gives me a gnaw."

"It scares you, Daniel?"

"I said it shakes me."

"Enough to quit the story?"

"You kidding? Go to bed, Cork. We kick off tomorrow with some hard phone duty."

Hard indeed. Corkie took a telephonic run at *The Washington Post* and gained, as she put it, an inch. The paper had run a story last year on *Red Alert* and had interviewed J.B. Hammermill. The background on the newsletter was necessarily sketchy. The thing hadn't been in publication more than a few weeks at the time of the interview, and Hammermill had been tight-lipped about details.

He offered the *Post* mumbo jumbo concerning a "vast network of highly placed informants" and was equally vacuous concerning the financial backing of his publishing venture. "All my own money. Some people bet on horses. I'm betting that enough people in this country are worried about the truth of the Commie

120

menace to support a publication that tells that truth bluntly, honestly, and without political considerations."

"Sounds like a throwback to the fifties," Dan commented, when Corkie came into his room to review her findings for him. He took another drag of carry-out coffee from the motel's Snak Shoppe and set the cardboard cup back on the table by the window.

"And he was just as vague as McCarthy, too, when it came to details about himself." She riffled her notebook pages. " 'I'm just a small businessman with a conscience.' Apparently, the reporter had written him off as a fringe looney at that point in the interview, because the story had no more to say about his background other than that he had been in various small publishing ventures in the past. Here and in the Midwest."

"How about the other local paper, the *Washington Times?* Replaced the *Star* a while back."

"Zilch. Same with *The New York Times.* That's no surprise, though. *Red Alert* has hardly made a national impact. *The Wall Street Journal* never heard of it, either. *USA Today* had one story filed on it; same kind of thing *The Washington Post* ran. No background on Hammermill. I guess their reporter felt like the *Post's.* Today's curiosity piece; tomorrow's non-news. The guy didn't give anything out on himself, but he came across as too insignificant to run a follow-up on. I know the feeling."

"You're pretty damned thorough for a gossip columnist, Cork."

"Lot of good it did. How are you doing?"

"What I've got makes what you've got sound like deep background. I talked Cousin Roy into checking Hammermill against NCIC and ViCap databases—"

"You can do that?"

"He can. But there's nothing there."

"Dead end?"

"How can a guy in the publishing business, even with a little rag like his, operate in a personal vacuum? Damned if I—" He snapped his fingers. "Wait a minute. Long shot, but worth a try."

"I'm not with you, Daniel."

"You wondered about the computer terminal setup in your sublease digs? Casey's a hacker who can make your garden variety computer op look like a two-fingered typist. How do you think I broke that series killer case?"

"She was in on that?"

"Zipped through federal computers as if they were public domain, Cork. Fort Worth runs an hour behind us, so she should still be in her hotel."

She was, and she wasn't happy. "Nice to hear from you, Daniel, my love, but what you're asking means I'll have to use a client's machinery. Also, what you expect me to do is more than slightly illegal. Unauthorized computer access is a criminal charge."

"That didn't stop you before, Casey."

"Chalk that up to the euphoria of trying out virgin equipment."

"You're my last hope on this thing."

"Same old line."

"It's true."

"Damn it, Daniel! I'm sitting here in a rumpled bed dying for coffee, hair like a rodent's reject, and you're asking me to break federal law."

"It's important. I'll call you back at five, okay?"

She sighed mightily. "Oh, God, all right. I'll try."

"Now what?" Corkie asked as he hung up.

"She's got to find a secure terminal and modem, then she'll try to access federal intelligence data bases."

"FBI and CIA?"

"That's just the beginning. There are a dozen of them. The armed services intelligence services, NSA, the

State Department Bureau of Research and Intelligence, Treasury's security unit, the White House Secret Service Detail. Quite a list. It'll take her a while."

"If she doesn't get her head cut off in the process. Where do you find such people?"

"Right across the hall. Come on, get your coat."

"Where are we headed?"

"Any place but here. To see the town, use up time, stall until five."

"Charlie would love this."

"Charlie won't know."

"Hope you had a nice day, Daniel." Casey's voice, some six hours later, was slightly metallicized by its satellite bounce from Fort Worth.

"Killed a lot of time in the Air and Space Museum and the rest of the Smithsonian." Charlie would have had a seizure. "And you?"

"I've had one hell of a day, thanks. I don't know why I keep doing things for you."

"What are neighbors for?"

"It's not easy to be one of yours. I just hope Elbasco Data, Inc., never finds out what one of its customer service terminals was doing between the hours of noon and three-fifteen this P.M."

"You blew lunch for me?"

"Only for you, Daniel. Couldn't have eaten anything, anyway. Some assignment! I couldn't get through FBI or any of the armed services safeguard codes. The CIA has some kind of tracer system. I think I backed out of Langley just in time. State, Treasury, and the White House were no go, either."

"A flop? You got nothing?"

"I didn't say that. A funny thing happened on my way to NSDC."

"National Security Data Corporation, right here in Maryland?"

"The same. The funny thing was that they're evidently in the middle of changing their Data Encryption Standard safeguard to a new algorithm, and I—"

"Casey, Casey, I don't have the remotest inkling what you're talking about."

"Oh. Well, it's as if you were changing the lock on your front door, and somebody just walked in during the change, at the point where there was no lock at all. I got something."

"I'm glad you're on our side, lady. You got what?"

"I got Hammermill, who isn't Hammermill at all. He's Alexander Graber Mahool." She spelled that while he scribbled furiously in his notebook. "Born Los Angeles, 1942. Public high school. Graduated from UCLA in 1963. ROTC in college, then army service. Seven months in Vietnam. All-American boy so far, but here's where he began to go off on a spur line. Got a medical discharge for mental stress. Then he began to show up at war protest rallies."

"A late-blooming flower child?"

"He wasn't anti, Daniel. He was rabidly pro. Worked for General Glendenning's wacko presidential bid. After that, he married a Gladwyn Coski, daughter of a small-time newspaper publisher in downstate Illinois. He worked for that paper until he was fired in a disagreement over some slanted articles he wrote. Held various jobs in right-wing candidates' political campaigns—which brought him to Washington. Started *Red Alert* eighteen months ago, but it's too insignificant to be his main source of income. That's all I could drain out of NSDC's data bank, my love."

"You're a Liberace of the computer keyboard, Case. I have no idea what all this means, but I don't feel quite so derailed now. Does it bother you a tad to be extricating classified tidbits?"

"Only if I get caught. Does it bother you that a private contractor to the government like NSDC is collecting personal data on private citizens?"

"Hell of a point. You be good, Case."

"Same goes for you. I hear Washington is wall to wall with frustrated congressional aides in skirts. Call me when you're lonely, Daniel, not just when you need a data thief."

"So now," said Corkie, after Dan had reviewed his expanded Hammermill file for her, "precisely what?"

"There's nothing precise about this. We're still flailing. But tomorrow, we'll take a flail at Mr. Hammermill-Mahool's *Red Alert*."

Assembling the funds had been a complex procedure. Winnie Stanfield had personal access to nearly two million dollars, but those dollars were in the form of fourteen high-grade stock issues, three major mutual fund holdings, and a substantial investment in a money market trust, with the balance in a scattering of more venturesome common stock holdings. The problem, Stanfield realized, was to assemble a cash package in the amount Hammermill had specified without leaving himself in an overly vulnerable position should there be a subsequent investigation.

When he decided to act, Stanfield had nearly twenty thousand in his several checking accounts. That had easily covered Hammermill's initial action. The income from his holdings in recent weeks had totaled just over forty thousand, with another seventy thousand in capital gains declared by one of the mutual funds. Right there was almost half of it. The balance came from judicious selling of several minor holdings through three brokerage houses, the withdrawal of a portion of the money market trust, and the addition of part of his last two federal paychecks. The problem was not one of availability of money. The trick was to extricate a quarter million dollars of it in a manner that would not ultimately set IRS bells clanging so loudly they would lead to a disastrous audit.

He thought he had managed it adroitly enough. Last night, the $240,000 balance due Hammermill had lain in his open eel-skin briefcase on the desk in his study. He felt the prickly aura that a mass of currency transmits to those in its proximity. Close to a quarter million in twenties, fifties, and hundreds was a *lot* of paper.

He snapped the briefcase shut, flicked off the desk lamp, and carried the money with him as he locked up. Upstairs, he slid the briefcase between the headboard of his double bed and the bedroom wall. Then he walked down the carpeted hall to Myra's room.

She slumped against her banked pillows, awkwardly leafing through a magazine with her left hand. He couldn't look at her, at the sling, at the bandaged and maimed right hand, without experiencing a hot rush of renewed fury.

"How do you feel, baby?"

She didn't hear him, didn't realize he was there, until he moved into her side vision. Damn, this was hard to take; harder still to remember to shout at her.

"How are you?" he called. How did you sound tender when you had to shout?

"I'm okay, Daddy." She did look better than she had when he'd driven up to New York to bring her home. The random network of facial cuts had faded to pinkish streaks. The sadistic bastards had packed their bomb with roofing nails and glass. Some of the fear had

126

faded from her wide green stare. But not all of it. Certainly not all of it. It never would.

The arm would heal. The missing little finger would be compensated for. Little fingers weren't essential. Maybe she would pass off the disfigurement as a badge of honor. You never knew with young people. But the hearing loss . . .

"Let's hope that an aid will help," the St. Vincent's intern had said to him while she had dressed. "Total hearing loss can be a more devastating setback than blindness."

"That I don't believe."

"Who can talk to somebody who's stone deaf?"

A chilling comment, that. But Myra's hearing had come back. A little. And they had an appointment with a D.C. otologist next week. Stanfield was doing what he could. None of this was remotely Myra's fault, or his. That was part of the hell of it. A madman an ocean and a continent away had pursued a demented obsession, and now Stanfield was personally impacted by that insanity. He was doing what he could, all right. The next step was to get the money to Griffin.

This morning, she had come downstairs to help him with breakfast, and he'd damned near wept as she tried to break the eggs one-handed.

"Want—" He had to stop, clear his throat, and try again. "Want some help?"

"What, Daddy?"

God *damn* that bloody son of a bitch! He slammed his fist on the kitchen table. "Help?" he said, much louder. "Do you want some help?" Unnerving how the need to shout restricted what you could say. All this because of a remote bastard in his gold and white uniforms thumbing his nose at the world. If he thought he was immune, he had one hell of another think coming.

127

Stanfield and his daughter ate in near silence, a damned disturbing enforced silence.

"You'll be all right by yourself until Mrs. Hutchins gets here?" he shouted. He was learning that she could grasp a conversation a little better if she watched his mouth as he spoke. He'd asked her that every morning, though he'd hired the LPN to stay with her from 9 A.M. until he arrived home in the evening.

"I'll be fine." She had begun to speak much louder herself, taking on a trait of the seriously deaf.

He drove his own slate gray Olds, having rejected the offer of a Secret Service agent. He'd felt less exposed as just another anonymous commuter. Now he was unencumbered by a two-legged Doberman to complicate his activities.

The morning sun reflected off the briefcase's leather sheen on the seat beside him. Maybe this was a naive way to transfer a quarter million bucks, but hadn't the Hope Diamond been safely delivered to the Smithsonian by nothing more elaborate than first class mail?

State Department security did not yet extend to the briefcases of management-level employees. Stanfield reached his office outwardly cool, but inwardly close to jittering with unexpected excitement. This was his final action on behalf of Swift Sword. What was to follow belonged solely to Hammermill. That was the beauty of it. The risk was predominantly Hammermill's, too. Stanfield could appreciate the attitude of the air force silo button pushers. Once the Minuteman was launched, the buttonmen were out of it. The missile took the risk of countermeasures. The missile did the killing.

. . . Took the blame.

Griffin appeared as Stanfield had requested, at nine-thirty sharp, with an empty briefcase of his own.

128

"No visitors, no calls," Stanfield instructed his little gray matron of a secretary, and he shut his office door.

His aide, he noted, tried hard to regard the bundled bills as just another pile of paperwork, but he swallowed a lot, as the two of them transferred $240,000 in cash from Stanfield's Gucci leather to Griffin's newly purchased pebbled black Samsonite.

"Is there a message?"

"The money is the message, Griff." Why did the man appear so damned nervous? Surely he'd known such a delivery was to be the final action in Swift Sword's activation. "What is it, Griff? Frigid feet at this late date?"

"No, no. I'm . . . not accustomed to handling large sums of money. My academic background, I'm afraid."

"Is that so?" Was that so? "Griff," he said pointedly, "a hell of a lot is riding on this. I'm certain you understand that."

"I do understand. But I'll admit I'll be relieved when my part in the project is completed."

Oh? Stanfield had thought the man was relishing his cloak-and-dagger role. Had something happened?

"What is it, Griff?"

The aide shot him a look that was oddly rabbity. "I've been . . . offered a position. In California."

"A Princeton man going to California? That's a little hard to believe."

"I haven't made up my mind yet." He snapped the latches on his briefcase. His bald pate glistened in the glare from the recessed fluorescents.

I wouldn't be too damned unhappy to have Griffin out of here, at that, Stanfield realized. Arrogance yesterday, sweaty obeisance today. Something is wrong with the man. But with Griffin safely pocketed in some obscure

129

university department three thousand miles west, Stanfield's link with Swift Sword would be neatly severed.

"Make the delivery," he told Griffin. "Then we'll talk."

The purpose of using the man at all had been to set up such an expendable linkage, Stanfield had come to admit, though at the time, he had rationalized the arrangement solely as one to avoid direct contact with Hammermill. That aspect had worked as planned. Hammermill knew Griffin only as "Mr. Johnson," bearer of the verbal proposal, then the carrier of the initial fee. Today he would be the agent for delivery of the full payment balance for the project's activation. All this on behalf of an anonymous source. Stanfield was protected by Griffin's positioning between buyer and contractor. He would be totally disassociated from Swift Sword by Griffin's departure from State.

"Yes," Stanfield resumed amiably, "let's have a talk about your California offer." He consulted his desk calendar. "Thursday morning would be good for me. You?"

"Fine. I'll look forward to it."

Stanfield saw him to the door.

And never saw him again.

Dan's day had begun sourly with, of all things, a fight at breakfast. In the motel's uninspiring cafe, Corkie had defied him. She was going her own way today, on a mission about which she was irritatingly vague. Wouldn't tell him a damned thing about it. She flatly refused to go with him on his excursion to *Red Alert* and to tag along in his effort to interview, he hoped, Hammermill-Mahool himself. She was going off on her own on *his* story, damn it!

He didn't like that at all. Her jaw set reminded him of Sandy, just before their marriage blew sky high:

adamant, willful, ultimately having her own way. Except that Sandy hadn't managed to keep personal insult out of it. At least Corkie hadn't stooped to that. She had just become Blauvelt's piece of the rock, and you can't win an argument with a rock.

She ended it with, "You take the car." Superfluous generosity, since he considered it his anyway. "Don't worry about me." Then she was gone in a phone-summoned taxi. She was using her own money. What the hell was she up to?

Okay, Corkie baby, I'll do my own thing, too. He returned to his room, dialed 212, and found Cousin Roy at his desk again. The slow season?

"Winter does help keep 'em off the streets. What's the deal this time?"

"An extension of the same favor, Roy. This time, run the name Mahool. Alexander Graber Mahool. Born in Los Angeles in 1942."

Dan spent the half-hour wait constructing mental scenarios and came out of it no better organized. Griffin had bought the nebulous protection of anonymity by tossing Dan Hammermill's name. Hammermill had checked clean, but had turned out to be an alias for no apparent reason.

Then: "Danny Boy," Roy's distant voice reported, "we lucked out and done caught us a wild goose. Alexander Graber Mahool has a rap sheet. Just one entry, but maybe it's got promise. He was busted by the LAPD four years ago for allegedly acting as a go-between in an alleged scheme to waste the President of Romania, when the pres was scheduled to visit L.A. on his goodwill tour."

"That's a lot of alleging, Roy."

"Because the thing never came off."

"The plan?"

131

"The L.A. stopover. It was canceled after Mahool's arrest. Then the charge was dismissed. Nothing came of it but the L.A. computer entry. If you hadn't told me he was from there, I wouldn't have gone there. NCIC and ViCap don't show anything on a Mahool, but their mainframes have some pretty big gaps still. You got something?"

"Nothing I can make work yet, Roy. But you'll be one of the first to know."

"I sure hope so, Cousin. My neck's getting stretched a little thin up here."

NSDC computers had missed that little tidbit, too. Maybe that was what came of hiring low bidders. But what did he have, Dan wondered? Nothing of substance, but maybe a playable chip. He smiled tightly. A chip in a game he didn't even know the name of.

The morning was fairly well shot by the time he rolled the Chevette onto the Capital Beltway. He shot it even deader by getting lost in the suburban mishmash that was College Park and/or Silver Spring and/or Chevy Chase. Everything in this part of the country ran together. The locals seemed highly loath to put up signs to tell a boggled reporter who'd made a wrong turn off the Beltway just where in hell he precisely was.

He should have bought a map. He stopped at a McDonald's to fortify the waning effect of the motel's coffee, added an Egg McMuffin to ballast his sour stomach, and found himself at brunch.

When he finally was pointed toward Rathmussen Tower by a service station attendant on cluttered Route 97, and nosed between the cracked paint stripes in the Rathmussen's thinly populated parking lot, he realized he was hitting the place at lunchtime. Mark of the rank amateur. Charlie, I'm sorry, but the damned woman insisted on unmaking my day.

132

The building either had never made it as a class address or had been sucked dry by the onslaught of overbuilt better space nearby. A quarter mile beyond the fringe of spindly pines at the far end of the parking area gleamed soaring steel and glass that made the Rathmussen's naked and water-stained concrete bunkerish by contrast.

The lobby was chilly, its fountain dry and peppered with brown leaves from a stand of dead ficus in a neglected planter. The security desk was unmanned, its implied authority emasculated by a layer of fine dust. The directory on the wall at the elevator bank showed a lot more blanks than white lettering of tenants who still hung on, probably enjoying bedrock rents. *Red Alert* was on the fourth floor. The elevator needed a broom job, but it worked.

The publication's frosted glass entrance was opposite the elevator. He knocked, then walked in. The girl in white wool knit clicking away at the word processor just inside the door didn't even look up.

"Mr. Hammermill?"

"Oh, dahm!" She made a correction, delicate fingers flying. Then she looked up. The sheer wool was prim, but it didn't hide a thing. Her orange scarf was a neat touch of daring color; hell of a contrast to the black sheen of her hair. Chinese maybe?

"He is just going to lunch." Her voice was small and low-pitched. "You have appointment?"

"No. Hoped I'd catch him in." Hoped to catch him by surprise.

"You wait." She nodded toward a hard chair across the tiny reception area and picked up her phone. Now he noticed the rainbow-hued plastic nameplate press-applied to the corner of her desk. Salesman's sample. *Francine Nguyen.* Not Chinese. Lovely profile, seen from

133

here. Smooth coal-black bangs, snubby nose, full mouth, skin like antique copper . . .

"He wants to know who you are."

"Dan Forrest, from *NewsLeak*."

She had a little trouble with that, then she covered the mouthpiece again. "He says *NewsLeak* or *News*—What?" she said into the phone. "Okay," she said to Dan, "Jimmy— Mr. Hammermill says go in, but make it short. He has appointment."

Jimmy?

Dan threaded through the cluttered workroom beyond, passed a chubby middle-aged woman behind a hedgerow of publications she was culling intently with scissors and Scotch tape, then he edged around a squeaky-clean youth with a near-military haircut who was making an electric typewriter sing. And he worked his way into the dusty dungeon of Mr. Hammermill-Mahool.

The single window, designed never to slide up or down its now oxidizing aluminum frame, wore the haze of neglect. The steel desk had an unmistakable government surplus look. A reference table was sludged with editorial detritus. The several chairs were the same unforgiving dark oak as their brother in the reception area. J.B. Hammermill's office seemed as much a back-to-the-fifties effort as apparently was his newsletter.

The man himself stood, not tall but conspicuously straight, behind his jumbled desk, hair short-cropped to a dated stiff brush the flat black of hair dye, mustache trimmed square, eyes hard black beads in the glare of the overhead tube.

"*Newsweek* or *NewsLeak*?" Hard voice, too.

"The latter."

"I thought so. I don't want to be interviewed by *NewsLeak*, Mr. Forrest was it? Not by a rag like yours.

God knows what you people would try to make out of *Red Alert*."

"I'm not here for a story on *Red Alert*, Mr. Hammermill. I'm working on something else altogether." Dan shut the office door behind him, a not so subtle hint to Hammermill that he was here for a more than casual purpose. "Can we sit down?"

Hammermill nodded coldly and sat, glancing at his watch. "Make it short. I've got a luncheon meeting."

"I'm working on the death of Marguerite Falconer."

"Falconer? Oh, the movie actress. Killed in New York, wasn't she? What brings you down here?"

"She seems to have had some Washington connections."

"Not with me, Forrest. Don't I wish! Look, I've got somebody waiting—"

"Your name was given to me by someone with a possible connection to the case." Try that on for size, buddy.

Hammermill's stony expression hadn't changed at all when Dan had mentioned Marguerite Falconer, but now his jaw muscles flexed. Just once; just a little. Just enough.

"Ridiculous!" he snapped. "Who?"

"I'm not at liberty to say." Fishing, fishing, but Dan had already caught something far more significant than a jaw muscle twitch. All right, Hammermill, here's another hook. "We understand that Falconer had something going with Edwin Stanfield."

"Who?"

Come on, Hammermill. "Under Secretary of State Edwin Stanfield."

Was that a glisten of moisture behind the mustache?

"Why would I know anything about that?"

"That's my question, Hammermill."

135

"You're way up the wrong tree, my friend. I run a little monthly newsletter that barely makes its own way. What in hell would I be doing that involved something like the U.S. State Department?" He glanced pointedly at his watch again. "Look, I've really got to get out of here, you understand? I'm late already." He shot to his feet without giving Dan a chance to respond, and grabbed his coat from a hook on the back of the door. Then he stood aside impatiently for Dan to go out ahead of him.

In the reception area, Dan stuck out his hand. "Thanks for what you were able to give me." Which was more than you think, sir. "I've got to make a call. Mind if I use the phone here?"

"Be my guest," Hammermill offered sourly as he left the office.

"You want me to place call?" the Oriental receptionist offered.

"No. No, thanks. That was just so I could say goodbye to you." His eyes skimmed her desk. "No brown bag? You eat lunch out?"

She reached in a drawer. "I have brown bag."

"How about hot coffee?"

"I drink water from ladies' room."

"That's no way to eat lunch. Let me buy you coffee, at least."

"We have coffee maker here."

"Oh, come on. I saw a place on the way here. A block away. You can tell me about *Red Alert*. It'll be good publicity. How many times do you get the chance to have coffee with a New York reporter?" Shameless, Daniel.

She glanced toward the workroom door. "I get only one half hour. But . . ." Her quick smile dazzled. "Okay."

136

He'd read her right. No prim and proper little lady, this one. Not so little, either. When she stood, they were eye to eye. And she radiated an aura that transcended right wing office work. "Jimmy," she had tagged Hammermill. Just a tiny slip, but it had told Dan a lot. That had been the first lapse of two made here in *Red Alert's* fusty offices. The other had been Hammermill's own.

"Killed in New York," he'd said of Marguerite Falconer. Operative word: killed. No one had yet refuted the accidental death verdict.

Noontime Washington was as cold as Maine, but Griffin was perspiring again, and he hated it. The damned briefcase on the floor on the passenger side seemed to pulse with imminent disaster. His mouth was as dry as flannel. He was having trouble swallowing. His hands were damp inside his gray calfskin gloves. At Sixteenth and New Hampshire, he had to brake suddenly for a car that cut in too close, and his leg shook on the pedal as uncontrollably as if he had been palsied.

Hammermill had designated a restaurant on Route 97 near Wheaton. The Cathay. Chinese. The last thing Griffin needed this particular day was highly spiced Chinese food. His stomach was already in turmoil.

God, he wasn't cut out for this. He really wasn't. He had enjoyed it for a time. Hell, be honest with yourself, Dudley: you reveled in it at first—the thrill of being in Stanfield's confidence, the idea of actually influencing history in a positive way, the heady planning talks, the intoxication of helping to put one of his very own published theories into direct action.

Then that damned reporter in his scruffy motel room had brought him eyeball to eyeball with the risk. And Griffin had wobbled. Wobbled? He'd crumpled, and he had seen himself for what he was—a naive college prof fueled by self-delusion.

Not anymore.

What he had told Stanfield this morning had been a lie when he'd said it, but now it was the truth. He had gone from the under secretary's office to his own phone and called Gene Atherton at Berkeley. Old Tiger Inn classmates could be useful lifelong, and Dean H. Eugene Atherton, Princeton '57, came through. Now there really was a position in California, only an assistant professorship, but the distance from this increasingly dangerous entanglement in Washington would more than make up for the decline in prestige. Thursday, Griffin determined, he and Stanfield would come to an amicable parting. Over the ensuing weekend, he would be out of Washington, pride demolished but skin intact.

The restaurant was wedged between a hardware store and a fashion boutique in the commercial sprawl of Wheaton's southern outskirts. Griffin found a barely large enough space on a side street two blocks distant. He wedged the Pontiac into it, hoping the local police wouldn't ticket him for the eighteen-inch gap between the curb and the car's rear wheels.

The two blocks in frigidly thin sunlight were the longest he'd walked in his life. If some daytime mugger were to snatch the heavy briefcase . . . He found himself eyeing the most innocent of passersby with an apprehension that grew into a hard knot between his shoulder blades. Just a few more minutes, craven Professor Dudley Griffin, and you will be forever free of this gathering nightmare, the misbegotten project you yourself named Swift Sword.

Inside the Cathay's hammered brass entrance portal was a knot of people waiting for tables. Beyond the

138

shuffling group, he spotted Hammermill already seated in a secluded corner.

Griffin shucked off his coat for the Chinese checkroom girl, but he held tightly onto the briefcase. Hammermill did not rise. Not for a messenger.

"The full payment?" He nodded at the case as Griffin sat and slid it toward him beneath the table. "Everyone directly involved is aware, I assume, that this delivery constitutes the final—and irrevocable, I might add—go ahead. You understand that? More importantly, your principal understands that?" A corner of his squared mustache lifted, a trifle disdainfully, Griffin thought. "What's your problem?" asked Hammermill.

God, did it show that blatantly? Into Griffin's galloping brain had just tumbled certain official wording he had tried to ignore since he had come across it in the welter of paper he'd processed for Stanfield. *"No person employed by or acting in behalf of the United States Government shall engage in, or conspire to engage in assassination . . ."*

Executive Order 12333. An executive order, Griffin was aware, constituted a voluntary restraint, not one legally imposed. He had theorized that a president could skirt around any legal problems of its violation by filing a secret national security directive that sanctioned direct action against a Kaddafi or a Sokolo.

But Stanfield was in no such position, and Griffin surely was not. Were Swift Sword to be exposed, even at this before-the-fact stage, they would be in violation of EO 12333. God alone knew what would follow.

Griffin had to get out of this. As promptly as possible.

Lunch was not pleasant. He ordered egg foo yung, typically unimaginative fare for an academic drowning in fear.

"What the hell is it, Johnson?" The man's dark-eyed stare ripped straight into him.

Griffin tried to keep it offhand. "Will you need me . . . further?" But a hot wave of apprehension rolled through him.

Hammermill's response was surprisingly mild. "I see no need for your continued participation. The operation is secure. Just go about your normal business and forget that you've had any part of Swift Sword." His voice was conversational, but his eyes were relentless. "The operation *is* secure, isn't it?"

Griffin cursed his moment of hesitation. He was a mile out of his depth, a lousy liar.

"Oh . . . yes. Certainly."

He would not go back to State this afternoon. Or tomorrow. That would give him time to close out affairs here, work out the remainder of his lease, arrange somehow to ship Juneau west, terminate his account at Equitable in Chevy Chase . . . A quick farewell to Stanfield Thursday, for form only. He didn't owe the man a thing. Stanfield had gotten him into this horror.

"Who else knows, Johnson, besides you and your principal?"

Who *else!* Hammermill had an unerring ability to slice directly to the core. "No one, for God's sake." Griffin forced another forkful of the spicy but suddenly tasteless egg patty.

"No one else at State?"

"No one." Then Griffin's stomach recoiled. He put down his fork with uncoordinated fingers. *At State,* Hammermill had said! But Griffin knew he had never—*never*—mentioned the State Department in any of their meetings. How had Hammermill known? How much more did he know? Was he aware of Griffin's true identity?

140

Griffin took a quick gulp of tea, unable to control the tremor as he raised the handleless cup. He didn't feel its scalding bite. He was conscious only of Hammermill's unblinking glare. Black animal eyes. Griffin had to get out of here.

"Sorry. I'm feeling a bit rocky today. We'll have to cut this short." He shoved his chair back and reached for his wallet.

"I'll get it, Johnson. You take care of yourself."

Without the briefcase, Griffin felt less exposed, but no less vulnerable. He retrieved his coat and shouldered into it awkwardly, as he pushed through the brass door.

Out on the sidewalk, the hard January air helped. At the corner, he stole a glance back toward the restaurant. Hammermill was nowhere in sight. I'm wildly overreacting, Griffin thought. But that didn't diminish his urgency to get out of Washington.

Hammermill watched "Johnson" claim his coat and hurry out the big brass entrance door. Mr. Dudley Griffin of the Farragut Arms Apartments on upper Connecticut Avenue was one frightened man. His name and address had not been at all difficult to acquire through his Pontiac's D.C. license plate, using one of the several key contacts Hammermill had cultivated since his arrival in the Washington area. And Griffin was surely hiding something that was of sufficient magnitude to have put him in a state of near paralyzing apprehension.

Hammermill hadn't been one hundred percent sold on "Mr. Johnson" as an intermediary from the outset. After he had followed him straight to the State Department, then I.D.'d the man from his license plate and accessed his background and current position, Hammermill had felt more confident. Edwin Stanfield, after all, was an under secretary of state. Hammermill wasn't

141

dealing with dabblers here. Yet Griffin was a man clearly out of his orbit, and he knew far too much for a man so obviously shaken. Too easy to break. Too damned easy.

Griffin had to go.

In his *Red Alert* offices fifteen minutes later, Hammermill unlocked the lower right-hand drawer of his desk, referred to a file card, and dialed a 212 number. He realized the call would show up on long distance telephone records, but the number was listed as the office of a free-lance editorial consultant, a logical enough call for a publication to place.

While the New York number rang three times, Hammermill wondered where Franky was. She hardly ever left the office at lunchtime. Then the New York end responded.

"Thorp," a mild voice said.

Behind the closed door of his undistinguished office, Hammermill said, "This is your D.C. client. I need you again."

Theodore Orpman had decided some years ago that his was no name for anybody who intended to make a living the way he was going to. He decided that right after he'd iced the mule with the big mouth a half-hour after that shambling idiot from Barranquilla had made what was to be his last delivery of Colombian snow.

The hit in the seedy Collins Avenue apartment over on the Beach had been no big deal; worth no more than the two Gs Orpman had been paid to do it. What rankled was the greasy attitude of the greasy man in the pink pants and white loafers who had delivered the money.

"We thank you, Thee-O-dore," the man had sing-songed. At that moment, Theodore Orpman had determined to get out of this steamy city that too often smelled of sour milk and sour death. He went north, to New York City, where he had a couple of contacts, and where he believed his future was at.

On the bus up endless 95, he worked on the name. His three navy years gave him the inspiration. The navy loved its partial word acronyms. COMINCH and CINCPAC and like that. Orpman . . . Theo Orp . . . Thorp? He liked it. "Thorp" had the impact of a silenced bullet.

At thirty-four, Thorp wasn't impressive in appearance. His taffy-colored hair was combed straight back from a pallid, high forehead. His eyes were the tint of gutter ice which, in closer look, gave the pupils a piercing intensity. He favored bland polyesters off the rack, a taste that abetted his near-invisibility in a crowd. He *looked* like an editorial consultant. Maybe just short of prissy; bookish, to be generous about it. Who would guess that he'd joined the navy one jump ahead of prosecution for a teenage street mugging in his native Miami?

Who would see past the wimpy facade that gave no hint of his navy SEAL background? He had been trained in the equivalent of the army's Special Forces techniques plus scuba expertise. The Vietnam thing had closed down before he'd gotten to use the training there, but he made use of a lot of it elsewhere after his enlistment was up. The scuba stuff hadn't come to anything, but the weapons training lived up to the recruiter's promise. It had prepared him for a civilian job.

He packed immediately after Hammermill's call. That was easy enough because his office was the front room of his apartment. The accommodations, business and personal, were no more than functional and would never have attracted even passing attention from the most desperate home decor feature writer. Except for a particular closet in the bedroom.

143

Following Hammermill's call, Thorp extracted a locking pin on one end of the clothes rod and swung the entire cantilever bar aside on its concealed anchor pivot. Behind it was the closet's blank wall. But the visible area was not a wall. With the toe of his left shoe, Thorp pressed a concealed release tab beneath the shoe rack. The left edge of the "wall" sprang outward, and he pulled it fully open.

The weapons concealed by the hinged panel fitted neatly into a restricted space on wooden support pegs. The firearms ranged from a tiny F.N. Baby Browning .25 automatic at the low end of the firepower scale up to an Armalite AR-18 5.56mm assault rifle as counterpoint at the high end. Between those extremes ranged a boggling array of the hand-held tools of Thorp's actual vocation. There was also a concise selection of alternative implements, and it was from these that he selected after a moment's deliberation.

Hammermill's information on Griffin had been succinct but adequate. Griffin, Hammermill had learned from the ostensibly irrelevant conversation that had served as nervous filler during their meetings, owned a dog— a big one. The fact of the dog and Hammermill's information on Griffin's address and working hours provided Thorp enough data to guide his special weapon choice.

He selected a surprisingly innocent-appearing item from the nonfirearms in his lethal collection, then carefully resecured the concealed door of the shallow cabinet.

The .45 caliber M-S Safari Arms Enforcer, a shortened version of the Safari Matchmaster, that nestled beneath his left arm in its fine-grained black leather holster, was not considered by Thorp to be a special weapon. It was as much a part of his standard dress as were his crepe-soled shoes. Only when he traveled by air did he forego the Safari Enforcer.

There would be no such problem this trip. In his own car, he could be in Washington by nightfall, pushing it just a little. Thorp wasn't lavish with his accommodations or his wardrobe, but he did invest in good machinery, as his closet armory attested. And his automobile. He drove a gunmetal blue Mazda RX-7 Turbo that had the lines of sleek power, though it was no BMW or Porsche. It was dependable and fast enough—0 to 60 mph in 6.7 seconds with its 182-hp, two-stage-turbocharged, intercooled, fuel-injected rotary engine. He would have preferred the Porsche 944 Turbo, but in his line of work, he never knew when he might be forced to abandon his suddenly hot vehicle, and the Mazda cost a full ten grand less than the Porsche would have. His ultimate dream was the BMW 325e, a rare beauty with a forty-five-thousand-dollar price. But he realized he would never be able to bring himself to abandon that baby, whatever the risk. So he had settled for the more expendable Mazda.

He left his building's basement garage on Manhattan's East Side nineteen minutes after Hammermill had called. Under a sunless gray wool sky, he wove skillfully through crosstown traffic to the George Washington Bridge. Once through the toll gate, the RX-7's fuel-injected turbo drummed smoothly southward on the Jersey Turnpike. Thorp's foot was heavy on the pedal, his ears alert for the first warning buzz from his radar detector. It was a new one, equipped to pick up even KR-11 shortpulse emissions.

10

HE HAD READ her right, Dan decided, as they sat at a tiny marble-topped wire table in a corner of the Wheaton sandwich shop, and he watched her take on a "Consultant's Special" club—a formidable triple-decked mound of Canadian bacon, melted cheddar, and cole slaw on dark Jewish rye. According to a pop psych article he'd read—had it been one of Melody Matso's in *NewsLeak?*—women who ate with enthusiastic abandon also went at more earthy pursuits the same way.

That's not the concern here, Forrest. He took a swipe at his grilled Swiss and chased it down with coffee from the shaving mug the shop affected, an unsettling, cutesy feature.

"So, tell me about your work with *Red Alert*." Innocuous enough?

"It is a job."

"Sounds interesting to me." Inspired, Forrest.

"If you think so." Her face was an exotic blank.

"How long have you worked for Mr. Hammermill?"

"A year."

Dan took another drag of coffee. A lovely bronze Sphinx. But she had called her boss "Jimmy." Tight-lipped Hammermill sure hadn't come across to Forrest as the type to encourage familiarity in the office. More here than meets the proverbial? Dan was betting on it.

"He's a good boss?"

That prompted an upward flick of the almond eyes, then she went back to the sandwich, somehow managing to attack the messy thing with unmessy style.

"Just the three of you put *Red Alert* together?"

"Three?"

"You, the chubby woman I saw in there, and Mr. Clean."

"And Mr. Hammermill. He uses what his wife finds in magazines and papers to make into his articles."

"His wife?"

"The—" She shot him a quick smile. "The chubby woman."

Ah-ha. This dusky lotus blossom doesn't mind a little twittery at Mrs. Hammermill-Mahool's expense. Add to that the implied intimacy of the Jimmy nickname.

"You're Vietnamese, Miss Nguyen?"

"So formal? 'Franky' is okay. Vietnamese and American. My father was American soldier. When war is over, I wait for him to bring me to America. But he never does. So I am adopted by other American people."

"When was that, Franky?"

"Nineteen seventy-five, when I am eight. I stay with them in Philadelphia until I am seventeen, then I leave before trouble with stepfather."

"Trouble?"

"You know. He thinks because I am woman now, I should be 'nice' to him. So I go, Mr. Forrest."

"Dan is fine. You went where?"

147

"From Philadelphia to Baltimore to work for company that had an ad in the paper for word processor people. I learn that in school. Then I come to D.C., first to work for Beltway Bandit in College Park."

"Beltway Bandit?" What the hell was that?

"Consultant along Beltway for government contracts. That's what they are called. Then I come to *Red Alert.*"

"Isn't that going backwards?"

She frowned. "Backwards?"

"From a government consulting firm to a minor newsletter publisher. The salary can't be an improvement."

"There are . . . other considerations."

Suspicions confirmed. Gorgeous young Afro-Asian assistant; fading, aging wife; arrogant boss-husband. Prime ingredients for an outside service arrangement.

"Is *Red Alert* the only interest Mr. Hammermill has?"

"You mean business?"

You're telegraphing, Franky. "What else?"

She looked down at her plate. "Just *Red Alert.*"

Dead end? He took the chance of blowing the whole interview. "What has he promised you, Franky?"

The delicately tilted eyes held his. "You think he promise me something? Why would he?"

Why wouldn't he? "Yes, I think so. You're a beautiful woman with a valuable technical specialty. You were moving up, then you took a lesser job with Hammermill's crank publication. Surely he promised you something more than working in a dusty office on the fourth floor of the Rathmussen building in Wheaton's backwater. What was it? To dump the worn-out wife and move you in?"

148

He waited. Ah, Charlie, the things you have me do. Would she jump up and flounce out of here? Shout at him in indignation? Maybe even slap him with those graceful fingers turned to hard brass?

. She didn't take any of those volcanic alternatives. Franky Nguyen just sat there and stared at her plate. Then she slowly raised her eyes, and he saw that her face had hardened.

"You say that I am stupid?"

"I didn't quite—"

"No, you are right. He uses me, but I use him, too. For raises, to maybe marry him. But I know in my heart he won't marry me."

"You actually love the guy?"

"To me, it doesn't matter. To be a wife is to have . . . to have . . ."

"Security?"

"Yes. Something I never have."

"So, you let him use you, knowing you probably still won't have it."

"It pays the rent." Pretty damned harsh pragmatism there. He'd just gotten his first inkling that something about Franky Nguyen wasn't being displayed at full face value. So far, she had come across as wise in her current worth as a commodity, but dumb as mud about her future. Or willingly blind to it.

"Let me tell you something." He wasn't conniving now. "I think your boss is into something unhealthy. I'd hate to see you get hurt. You know damned well he can't be making a living off that little newsletter of his. What else has he got going?"

"How should I know? And why should I say a damned thing to you, a reporter?" She had suddenly dropped the naive immigrant lilt he realized she'd been affecting. Now she came across as hardcore American. The switch was startling.

"Your name won't be mentioned." He had to quit spreading all this immunity around. He wouldn't have anyone left to quote.

"No, I don't want to be a part of what you might write. Thank you for lunch."

She began to get up, but he grasped her hand. And lowered his voice. "Listen hard, Franky. You're sleeping with a guy who I think is tied in with the death of Marguerite Falconer."

"Falconer?"

"The actress. Dead in New York last week."

"You think Jimmy—Mr. Hammermill had something to do with *that?*"

Was he making one hell of a mistake here? "It's a possibility. Look, he's using you like a toy. He'll throw you away like a toy. He's in his forties, respectably married, runs a right-wing newsletter. You think a guy like that would dump his middle-aged wife and marry a young woman like you?" A guy like that very well might, but she went for it.

"You mean marry a half-yellow, half-black woman like me?"

"I didn't say that."

"Yes, you did." But her eyes held no anger. "You're right, too. I'm only kidding myself."

He let her hand go. She took a long swallow of her hot chocolate. Then she said, "You really think he's . . . dangerous?"

"You should know better than I. What *do* you know about him?"

"He's from the Midwest. He worked on papers there. He takes care of his body. He's still a young man . . . that way. He can be good to me, and he can be mean, too. Last time, he . . . was angry because I pushed him to think more about our getting married, reminded him that he'd promised. He told me to keep my mouth shut or he would shut it for me. I knew then that I've been a little afraid of him since the beginning."

"Has he ever told you that he's not J.B. Hammermill, not Jimmy. He's Alexander Graber Mahool, not from the Midwest originally, but from Los Angeles?"

She appeared genuinely surprised. "Why would he change his name?"

"A little matter of an arrest for conspiracy to murder. But the charges were dropped."

She thought that over. Then she said, "Yes, I think he is into something more than *Red Alert*. Phone calls behind his closed door, which is usually open. Unexplained meetings. I let him believe I'm a simple foreigner who doesn't notice things like that. And there's the file box."

"File box?"

"A green file box. He keeps it in his desk, in a locked drawer. Once when I went in his office, he quickly hid it in the drawer. He thought I didn't see that."

"Maybe it's just a file of people who send him stuff for his newsletter. *The Washington Post* reported that he claims a whole network of correspondents who mail in items."

"No, I keep that list on a floppy disc for the word processor. It's a special mailing list for payments when he buys something they send in."

"Then what do you think he's got in that drawer?"

She shrugged delicate shoulders, and he knew in that moment that he had to get a look at that damned box.

"You have a key to *Red Alert's* office?"

"Yes."

"What kind of security does the building have?"

Franky put her cup down slowly. "You're thinking of breaking in there?"

"Well, I'm not going to ask you to take a shot at his locked desk drawer, and I'm not going in there during working hours. So, what it boils down to is, yes, I am thinking of breaking in there—if that's the right term. What kind of security does the building have?"

"The tenants there now can't afford the money for security. There isn't any at all."

Dan bit the end off a cold french fry. "Just the three locks, then? The building, the office, the desk drawer. How many can you help me with?"

"I don't want to be a part of this."

"He'll never know. Can you leave your office key where I can find it?"

She looked out the window onto busy Route 97.

"Look, Franky, I've told you that he's not who he says he is. He called the Falconer thing a killing, while the New York police still have it on record as an accident, and he's got a tie to the State Department through the assistant of a man there who's been linked to Marguerite Falconer. Put all that together, and your Jimmy is not the kind of guy you want to be all this involved with. I still don't know exactly what I've got here, but you can help me put it in clearer focus."

She wouldn't meet his eyes.

"The man threatened you, Franky."

She let out her breath in a long sigh. "I could put the key behind the fire extinguisher in the hall near the office. But I don't have a key to the building."

"I saw a side exit door to the left of the elevators. It has a panic bolt—opens only from the inside. Can you wedge the latch?"

152

"I'll try. But I can't do anything about the desk drawer lock. He keeps the key with him."

"When do you . . . see him again?" With this kind of thinking, Forrest, *NewsLeak* is surely your niche.

"Not 'til next week."

"Too much time. I'll have to take a chance without the desk key."

"When?"

"What the hell? Tonight."

"You're scaring me." Franky's voice was close to a whisper, and now her golden cheeks were underlaid with chilled gray. "So much could go wrong. It's not . . . professional."

"You've got a point there. I'm a professional reporter, I hope, but a raw recruit at cat burgling. You think of a better way, and I'll sure listen."

"I'm going to start looking for another job."

"Well advised. If I'm lucky, and if I'm right, there might not be one there much longer anyway. Until then, don't let him suspect anything."

Superfluous advice, but Franky didn't let it pass. "That," she said, "is mostly up to you, isn't it?" Then she opened her purse and with fingers that trembled, she dropped cold metal into his palm. "Take my office key now. But don't forget to leave it behind the fire extinguisher for me." She gave him a bitter little laugh. "I want him to think I'm a dumb immigrant in love with him, and he wants me to think he's an honest businessman tired of his wife. Two actors fooling themselves more than each other."

"There's a lot of precedent for that," Dan said gently. "The trick is to cut your losses and get out in time."

When he let her out of the Chevette at Rathmussen Tower's entrance, she ducked back in. "If you get caught—"

"Don't even think it."

He headed back toward the Capital Beltway, realizing that the essentially dumb stunt he intended to pull had the potential to land them both in scalding water.

He bought the oversized screwdriver in a Wheaton hardware store and the flashlight in a K mart near Largo. Purchased together, he thought, the two items might add up to something a little too significant to an alert clerk. Purchased separately, they pointed only to Harry Homeowner picking up basic needs.

When he got back to the motel, there sat Corkie downing a cheeseburger in the bare-bones coffee shop.

"Sorry about this morning," she said pleasantly. "I think I piqued too soon." She nodded at his two paper bags. "Shopping spree?"

"For tonight's entertainment. Where in hell have you been?"

She shot a glance around the drab restaurant, empty except for the disinterested, adipose-armed waitress wiping the counter at the other end of the room. "Sit down, Daniel." She leaned close, and her voice dropped. "I rented a car and went to Fairfax."

"*You* rented a car? Charlie will—"

"Oh, damn Charlie! I used my own money."

"Why'd you go off on your own? Why Fairfax?"

"Because I want to contribute to this story, not just tag along. And Fairfax is where Stanfield rents a house."

"How'd you find that out?"

"With one confused telephone company billing clerk—that was me, and one highly courteous secretary

154

eager to straighten out an address mix-up—she was Stanfield's. Result: his Fairfax address."

He had certainly underestimated his traveling companion. "Clever, Cork, but what made you assume he'd be home? Was he?"

"Of course he wasn't. But his daughter was. She was hurt in the Penn Station bombing, remember?"

"She's the one you wanted to interview? For what?"

"Come on, Daniel. We were stonewalled by Stanfield at State. His aide came unglued when you linked Stanfield with Falconer. If the man's into something heavy, who would be more likely to notice than the only woman in the family? His wife's dead."

He had really underestimated her.

"The wire stories said she was in seclusion to recover from serious injuries. Not in a hospital; in seclusion. Where does one logically seclude? At home, Daniel. Ergo, I went down there to talk with Myra Stanfield."

"And?" The damned woman had him by the nose.

Corkie had talked her way past the LPN Stanfield had on duty when he wasn't. And she had convinced Myra that she was from a woman's magazine doing an article on how families coped with sudden catastrophic stress. No names would be used; incidents would be disguised.

"Now you're doing it, too. We're spreading anonymity assurances around like they're soap samples. So what did you get?"

"A tough interview. She's missing a finger, but her arm's coming along. Her hearing is in really bad shape. What I got, though, was the distinct impression of an infuriated father, obsessed, she believes, with somehow getting back at the guy who did all that damage to his baby."

"Sokolo?"

"That's what she said."

"She have any specifics?"

"No, but a strong gut feeling from various things he had said and from the way he was acting."

"What way?"

"A little on the furtive side, from what I could gather."

Dan gazed unseeing at the bored waitress behind the distant counter. "Somehow I feel that we've got our hands on most of the pieces of the Falconer story, but they just don't quite fit together. Hammermill could be the key."

She nodded at the paper bags he'd set on the table. "Presents for the folks back home?"

"I'm going to visit Hammermill's desk tonight."

"And the keys are in those bags?"

She sure caught on fast.

"I figure I—"

"We, Daniel."

"Come on, Corkie."

"Damned if I'm going to sit on my butt in my room and reorganize notes while you're having all the fun, breaking and entering."

"If I'm lucky, it'll be entering and breaking." There wasn't any way around this woman. He explained the setup.

"It's a long shot, Daniel. A stupid, risky, hare-brained long shot."

"That's why you ought to stay put right here."

"No, that's why you couldn't keep me away with anything less than phenobarbital."

His eyebrows went up speculatively.

"You wouldn't!"

No, he wouldn't. So they drove to the Rathmussen Tower together.

*　　*　　*

Thorp had parked the Mazda on a Chevy Chase side street just off Connecticut. From here, he could comfortably watch the front entrance of the Farragut Arms Apartments, his line of sight just skimming the top of the yew hedge that rimmed the large private home on this side of the wide avenue. Well-kept evergreens on both sides of the street shielded him from possible curious eyes in the secluded corner residences. A good setup. If a cop chanced by, he had his cover story ready. Waiting for a friend to arrive on the bus, Officer. The stop was nearby.

He'd been here since 4:55, early dark on this dreary mid-winter afternoon. He hadn't seen Griffin come home from work, but he would have missed him if the man commuted by car and had driven in the rear entrance of the apartment's underground garage. Thorp had noted that access on his reconnaissance swing around the building, before he had staked it out from here.

He chewed absently on the last piece of Roy Rogers chicken he'd picked up on the way in and washed it down with the last of his coffee. He stuffed the wrappings back in the bag and dropped the bag on the floor in the back. He kept the empty cup and its top on the seat beside him. If this waiting went on for a while, he'd need it.

The possibility that Griffin had entered the apartment building unobserved was of no concern. Thorp had based his plan on the dog. A Samoyed, Hammermill had told him. Big dogs like that needed exercise, especially after a day cooped up alone in an apartment. And in this neighborhood, with the fast-moving traffic on Connecticut, it was unlikely that a valuable dog like that would be allowed to run off a leash.

At 6:30, the traffic thinned and made Thorp's across-the-avenue surveillance easier. He was certain he hadn't missed Griffin, but his eyes had been wearied by the vehicular crisscross between his vantage point and the building's ornate brickwork entrance. It was the only bright area in the surrounding darkness, illuminated by the orange glow of twin wrought-iron lanterns that flanked the heavy stained-wood doorway.

At 6:51, a man in a black overcoat stepped out, a leash in his hand, and held the door for a reluctant . . . what? Thorp came instantly alert.

A wolfish muzzle poked out of the doorway's shadow into the soft light of the lanterns, sniffed the cold night, then stalked out.

German shepherd. Could Hammermill have made a mistake about the breed? He came close to following the man and his shepherd, then he realized that, if Hammermill had been accurate, Griffin could very well slip out of reach, while he, Thorp, followed the wrong man.

He forced himself to sit back and continue his concentration on the entranceway. At 7:03, the man in the black overcoat led his German shepherd back in, standing politely aside to let a middle-aged couple enter ahead of him.

At 7:15, Thorp began to feel his first little tweaks of doubt. Too quick. Hammermill had wanted him to do this too damned quick. Thorp hadn't had the time to research this hit himself. He'd had to act on Hammermill's info. Too much room for error with secondhand info. Too much error already: Hammermill's for not giving him enough time; his own for accepting that.

At 7:17, the apartment building's entrance opened, and an impatient dog bounded down the steps to be brought up short by its leash. A big dog. Pure white. Pricked ears and a curled plume of a tail. Samoyed. Behind the eager dog, carefully closing the big door, was a tall man—Hammermill had said Griffin was tall, his height accentuated by his velvet-collared gray chesterfield and an incongruous Pakistani-style fur hat.

Thorp opened the car door. Ninety-eight percent sure. He slid the ten-inch-long metal tube assembly from beneath his seat and carefully worked it into the left sleeve of his black storm coat. The assembly was short enough to allow him to bend his arm with the protruding end of the mechanism icy against his wrist. He locked the car, waited at the corner for a northbound cream-colored limo to pass, then strolled across Connecticut.

The man with the Samoyed had walked north, away from Thorp. At the corner, he led the dog to the right, into the next darkened side street. Thorp, trailing him by two hundred feet, quickened his steps.

When he turned the corner, the man and dog were halfway down the short block. Thorp paced them. At Delaware, the narrow back street paralleling Connecticut, man and dog paused. Then they turned north again, away from the Farragut Arms into residential shadow along a sidewalk deserted on this raw night.

Thorp felt a dampness in the air. A foretaste of snow? He raised his mouton collor awkwardly with one hand. The tube was still cold all along his left arm. When he reached Delaware, he turned north to follow the man with the Samoyed. He was still ninety-eight percent sure this was Griffin plodding along in front of him, the leash taut under the dog's impatient pull. But Thorp was as careful a contractor as he could be under always tense circumstances.

When he was five paces behind, he called pleasantly, "Mr. Griffin?"

The man stopped, turned. The dog looked up from the leafless lawn-side shrub it had been sniffing. Then it trotted to Thorp, jumped and planted its forepaws

159

against his chest. A dog in love with everybody. Thorp rubbed the heavily furred neck with the chilled fingers of his right hand.

"I thought I recognized you, Mr. Griffin. I'm Ed Granby. Live across Connecticut. The missus and I get a kick out of watching you walk the dog. Beautiful animal."

"Thank you," the man said stiffly.

"He's a Samoyed, right, Mr. Griffin?"

"That's right, but he's a she." He tugged at the leash. "Come on, Juneau."

"Have a nice evening," Thorp said affably as he strode past. Three times he had used the name, and there had been no correction or denial. The man was Griffin.

Five paces ahead of his target, Thorp slid the metal assembly from his sleeve and detached the tubular protective sheath. He shielded these actions with his body. No one was on the sidewalk ahead. There was no traffic on this isolated street. He stopped; turned. The sidewalk was empty behind them as well. He centered the device on Griffin's chest and pressed the release.

There was very little recoil or sound, comparable to the tiny kick and metallic twang of a spring-fired pellet gun.

As if he'd walked full tilt into a wall, Griffin's shoulders hunched in abrupt reflex. He stumbled backward. He clutched his chest with both hands as he fell. His head hit the sidewalk with a louder whack than the weapon had made.

The dog leaped away to the limit of its leash, which was still looped around Griffin's wrist. The hat rolled off. She moved back in, tail dragging in confusion, and nosed his bald head. She sniffed the hat, then she sank back on her haunches and watched Thorp approach.

160

He bent down and, with a sharp tug on the cylindrical hilt, pulled the projectile from Griffin's chest. It had penetrated overcoat, suit jacket, shirt, and undershirt to bury itself in his heart.

Thorp started to wipe the blood on the expensive chesterfield, glanced at the passive dog, grinned and cleaned the weapon on her thick shoulder fur. He needn't have concerned himself with the dog, after all; could have used a simpler weapon. The Samoyed had proved no threat—only a means of identification of Thorp's hit.

He enjoyed little touches like the defiant blade cleaning. He'd had the chance to do a real job on the Falconer woman. Diversion Hammermill had wanted, diversion he got. In the Chelsea Carlisle, Thorp had used a silk rope and handcuffs and the lipstick mumbo jumbo to keep the cops hopping. This job was simpler. The dog's bloodied fur was no more than a token, compared to the Falconer hit. A small signature.

Less than twenty seconds had elapsed from the time he had pressed the release. Thorp dropped the weapon's steel components into the pocket of his storm coat, then reached down again to slip his fingers beneath Griffin's coat and into his suitcoat pocket to slide out the man's billfold. He pocketed the billfold, then strode out of the shadows, retraced his steps along Delaware and the side street, recrossed Connecticut, and returned to his car.

The Samoyed whimpered, crouched down close to Griffin's head, and rested her muzzle between her paws. He had been hit with an American-improved copy of a ballistic knife issued to the elite Russian Spetsnaz forces — a heavy, spring-propelled Rockwell 56 blade that was deadly accurate for thirty feet. Thorp had purchased it legally in a New Jersey gun shop where it had been on prominent display, along with Oriental nunchaku articulated fighting sticks and shuriken throwing stars. No

161

permit required. He tested it in his apartment. From a distance of just under twenty feet, the four-and-a-half-inch blade of the projectile rammed through an inch and a quarter of the Manhattan White Pages—all the way to the four pages of Johnsons.

Thorp started the Mazda's engine and drove north toward the Connecticut Avenue interchange on the Capital Beltway. He wasn't going back to New York tonight. He'd find a motel along the Beltway, check in with Hammermill by phone tomorrow, after Hammermill would have heard or read the inevitable report of Griffin's death at the hands of a mugger—surely no novelty on nighttime streets in suburban Washington. Thorp realized he had probably removed all of Griffin's identification when he had taken the billfold, but the Samoyed wore a collar and license tag. The police would surely trace the dog's license number.

He followed the green and white Beltway signs off Connecticut Avenue into Kensington Parkway, then accelerated up the eastbound access ramp at Beltway Exit 33. At almost the same moment, Dan Forrest and Corkie Brion turned off the Beltway at Exit 31 into Georgia Avenue, Route 97, northbound toward Wheaton.

Dan pulled the Chevette into a parking slot near the fire door at the rear of Rathmussen Tower. The lot was as black and empty as the night sky. The air held that peculiar damp chill that told him snow might not be far off.

Corkie got out of the little car with him. He had debated with himself and decided not to leave her alone out here in the deserted lot. What he had tried, one more time before they'd left the motel, was to tell her to stay there. That was a laugh, like using hard words to stop a bulldozer at full throttle. Now, though, in the night's cold bite, she shivered a little.

"You still want to be part of this?"

"It's illegal and immoral, Daniel, but at least it's not fattening. Let's get it done."

In the deeper shadow of the building, he slipped the screwdriver blade between the jamb and the edge of the flush steel panel. Had Franky carried out her part of this, or would he snap the blade against a panic bolt still anchored in place? He pressed the screwdriver's plastic handle sideways.

It was like trying to move a boulder with a teaspoon. God damn it! Franky had been all talk. Lost her nerve, blew the—

The door yielded, just enough for him to jam the blade on through and use the heavy shank to lever the door open so he could hook his fingers around its edge. They were in.

The lobby was shadowed by the wan glimmer of a safety light beyond the neglected fountain. Their shoes crackled on floor grit. The building was dying, and whatever token maintenance service it still had used, they obviously didn't give the place top priority.

Twin rectangles of pale yellow extended across the lobby floor from the open elevators. They could have saved a few bucks there, but management was probably too preoccupied with finding a way out of here to worry about niceties like turning out elevator lights.

Just outside the front windows he saw only darkness. A hundred feet farther, the dim glow of downtown Wheaton silhouetted the hardscrabble pines at the edge of the visitors' parking area. He eased out of the fire door's shadowed recess, and he felt Corkie's breath on the back of his neck all the way to the elevator bank.

163

The elevator door took forever to slide shut. Would a passing security patrol notice just a single elevator was still down there? Maybe they should have taken the stairs.

What security patrol?

He didn't know whether to keep the elevator up here on the fourth floor or send it back down, so there would be the customary two visible in the lobby while he worked up here. Come on, Forrest, visible to whom? He was no good at this. His knees were unreliable, and he sure could use a men's room.

No time for that. He'd had Franky's key in his palm since they'd gotten into the elevator. It fitted *Red Alert*'s frosted door, turned easily. They slipped inside.

The hall had been minimally lighted with another low-watt safety bulb. In here, away from the dim rectangle of the door's glass, the darkness was near absolute. Dan shielded the flashlight's lens with his fingers and snapped it on.

Not quite soon enough. Behind him, Corkie barged into something that sounded solid and immovable. She spit out a couple of words he hadn't heard her use before.

"Sorry," she muttered. They waited in silence that yielded only more silence. The building was deserted, wasn't it? What were they waiting for?

Hammermill's desk had a locked drawer, lower right. Check, Franky. Nothing fancy about it, just the standard built-in two-bit lock on a government surplus desk. But he had never tried to crack one, until now.

He inserted the screwdriver blade in the slot between the top of the drawer and the crosspiece that supported the drawer above it. He slid the blade sideways. It thudded against the lock's upthrust bolt.

He handed the flash to Corkie. "Careful! Keep the beam away from the window." On his knees, he could see the damned bolt, a half-inch-wide strip of steel. Why had he thought this was going to be easy?

"Let me try." Corkie gave him back the light, dredged the cloth handbag she carried, and came up with a nail file. It turned the key slot nicely, but that didn't do a thing to the rest of the assembly.

Dan pressed down on the drawer pull. "There's a fair amount of play here. Maybe . . ." He gave her the flash again, slid the screwdriver back in the space above the drawer, and bore down on the handle.

The space widened. He pressed down with both hands. The drawer creaked.

"Pull it!"

Corkie tugged. Something gave, and the drawer popped open.

"Damn, Daniel! It's empty!"

And so it was. Then she lowered the flash to angle the beam farther inside. No, it was not empty. Her sudden tug had shot the contents against the drawer's back. Dan pulled out the metal file box. Green. Check, Franky, again.

"Looks like a recipe file," Corkie said. And it could have been picked up at any stationery counter, along with its tabbed separator cards. They were green, too. Hammermill used military filing, the cards in place ahead of the appropriately lettered separator.

> *Auden, H. d'A.*
> *1151 N. Beckman St.*
> *Farmington, MA 01421*

So read the first handwritten white card, along with a 617 area code phone number. This could be a subscription list, Dan thought as he thumbed through the cards, a list of key *Red Alert* recipients who might be worth dunning for contributions. Or a Christmas card list.

It could be, but it wasn't. Not with the penciled notations on the bottom of each card. *Spec. Fcs, US A, 68-71. B-trps, misc. expl.,* read Auden's card.

"I get 'miscellaneous explosives,' " Corkie said in his ear. "What's that other? Booby traps?"

"My guess, too. Auden's a U.S. Army Special Forces vet, three years service, with attendant skills."

Crouched on the floor beside her, Dan flipped through the cards slowly. More *misc. expl.,* a lot more. And *exp. w/ M-14, M-16* and *sm. arms spec.* and *commctns spec., chem. wpns. spec.,* and upwards from that to *exp. w/ M-47 Dragon.*

"Which is what?" Corkie's voice was uncharacteristically subdued.

"It's a shoulder-fired antitank rocket. Some recipe box! All the ingredients for mayhem."

"And barely coded."

"Tells us something about its keeper, doesn't it? This is the file of an arrogant, overconfident nut." Dan flipped through the last cards in the alphabetical sequence. "Hell of a collection. I'd guess he's— What's this?" He pulled out two cards clipped together with a slip of paper added.

" 'Swift Sword'?" Corkie read from the slip.

"These were behind the other cards, as if he'd pulled them out for—"

"For Swift Sword, whatever that is."

Dan pulled off the clipped-on slip. "*Woodman Arms,* with an Arlington address. The second one is just *Thorp,* with a New York City phone number." On the bottom

166

of Thorp's card was the notation, *US N SEAL, 73-76, spec. in elmntn.* What in hell was *"elmntn"?*

"Element something," Corkie offered.

"Elam, elem, elim . . . God, how about 'elimination'? My bet's that he's a hit man!" Dan copied that data, too. "These could be old business he forgot to refile. Or they could be something."

"Could be a dumb-head hobby, Daniel. All of it."

"Could be. Let's not press our luck here. We've laid a ton on it already. Time to get out of this place."

So far, they'd run a slick operation, Dan assured himself. But when they shut the drawer, again using the screwdriver to lever the extended bolt below the upper-drawer support then into place, he saw what had so cooperatively yielded before. The crossbar was bent upwards just slightly. Hammermill might not notice that. But the crimp the screwdriver had made in it would need a metalworker to conceal.

"So he notices it, Daniel. So he knows he's had a visitor. So what?"

"So, if there's no other evidence of a break-in, he can figure out that it was an inside job. His staff people—his wife and Mr. Clean—saw me leave with Franky. Then, a few hours later, his desk is pried open, but the office door . . . We got a problem."

They stood in the silent darkness, Corkie waiting for him to take the lead. "What would *The New York Times* do?" she asked.

"*The New York Times* wouldn't be here. *News-Leak*'s here. Let me have the flash." He yanked open the other four drawers of the desk, rifled them messily, and left them ajar. Then he knocked some of the papers off the reference table. In the outer office, he shuffled through filing cabinets and left them shuffled. He made a point of going through Franky's desk, too, and making it obvious that he had.

The final touch was to use the screwdriver's handle to break the glass on the entrance door from the hallway side. That made a hell of a crash up here, enough to start new sweat all around. Unnecessarily, of course, because they both were sure by now that they were the only people in the building. He left Franky's key behind the extinguisher in its wall recess, where she'd asked him to leave it. He wondered about her reaction to-morrow morning when she would walk into the mess they'd left.

In the elevator Corkie said, "I wonder what we got?"

He didn't have a definitive answer, but something chilling was sure pushing him close to one. The current order of business was getting out of here, which shouldn't be so difficult. Yet he had begun to feel as if he'd swallowed a lump of ice that wouldn't melt. It had lodged in his gut when he'd opened the file box and read a couple of the cards. And he knew it wouldn't go away by itself.

The elevator door opened on the still-deserted lobby. What was he worried about? He even remembered to pry the wad of paper out of the fire door's bolt recess and shove it into his pocket.

The night air hit them like pure oxygen. They both were high on it in seconds, elated that they had gotten away with—

Then Dan's blood chilled to ice water. Beyond the northwest corner of the building, an unseen vehicle threw a path of white light along the parking area's macadam. It grew brighter.

"Into the car, quick!"

For a heavy woman, she moved remarkably fast. They made it just as the car nosed slowly around Rathmussen Tower and swung its dual beams along the pavement behind the Chevette.

"If we duck down—"

"No." He'd seen the racked roof lights. "It's a police unit. They'll check a car pulled up like this to the back of a building at night." He'd been none too bright after all, he realized. Should have had Corkie drop him here, then come back at a stated time to pick him up. But that would have had its risks, too.

In the overhead mirror, he watched the prowl car slow. Then it stopped. The passenger side door opened. That meant there were two of them—one to check, one as backup in the car.

Dan grabbed Corkie's shoulder, pulled her to him and threw both arms around her. She squealed in surprise, just as his mouth closed on her cold lips.

Then she caught on. Her arms slid along his shoulders. Her palms pressed his head to hers. Hell of an actress. Her lips weren't so cold as they began to part.

. . . And the cop tapped his flashlight on Dan's window.

"Hey, in there, open up. Montgomery County Police."

Dan rolled down the glass. "Look, Officer, this is pretty damned embarrassing. If my wife ever found out I was—"

"Ain't you a little old for this kind of parking, sir?" The cop was a redhead with heavy sideburns and splayed teeth.

"He's not, believe me," Corkie said with a suggestive smile. "But I sure do wish he'd get a bigger car."

The cop allowed himself a tight smirk. "It's damned dangerous using a parked vehicle these days, friends.

169

Not like when you were a young stud, know what I mean? I don't need a couple of neckers mugged—or worse—on my shift, particularly in an out-of-town car. Don't complicate my paperwork, okay? Get the hell out of here, will you? Find yourselves a motel."

Dan started the engine. "Thanks, Officer. What do you say, Cornelia?"

She offered that lascivious grin again, and the cop stood back. Dan got the Chevette out of there, and neither of them said a word until they were back on Route 97.

Then Corkie shrugged. "We *are* going to a motel, Daniel."

"Don't push it."

"Didn't you feel anything at all?"

He had, damn it. He actually had. She'd been responsive and . . . comfortable.

"Dan?"

"Okay, so I felt a little something. But this is an assignment, and it's getting more and more complex. Maybe dangerous. If we were to. . . . Well, it would change and complicate and get in the way."

"I suppose. But at least admit that a fat girl could be—"

"Okay, okay, agreed. A fat girl could be."

It was then, at the intersection of 97 and Belvedere Boulevard, that the snow began. At first, it was no more than a silvery twinkle in the Chevette's headlight beams. By the time they reached the Barren Hilton, it looked as if it was settling into a real fall.

She gave it one more try. He had flipped on the bolted-down TV set, but he stood with his back to it at his single window, watching the clinging flakes begin to round the contours of the cars in the lot below. He liked snow back in Manhattan, where it brought a sense of

170

crisp order to the city. But now it seemed as if it were hurriedly trying to blanket something sinister.

"You feel it, too?" Corkie startled him, coming in so silently and standing so close in her blue housecoat. She sure loved blue. She had combed her hair shiny smooth and scrubbed her face clean of make-up. That gave her a vulnerable, naked look. He felt an unexpected stirring.

"Daniel . . ." She smiled, and her eyes glistened.

He was right on the edge of irretrievably blurting, "Oh, what the hell?" when the words from Channel 4 cut through everything.

". . . Griffin was an employee of the State Department. Montgomery County Police believe he was a victim of a mugging early this evening. The body was found by a passing motorist about 8 P.M. Griffin suffered a single stab wound to the heart, and his wallet was missing. Dudley Griffin, U.S. State Department, dead of a street crime at age fifty-one."

The ice lump was a lot bigger now, and Dan said in a peculiarly hoarse voice, "My God!"

11

WORD OF Griffin's death ricocheted through State as fast as news of an impending pay cut would have, but pay cut news would have had a longer lasting impact. "Dudley Griffin was, after all, one of us," said an assistant secretary to his administrative assistant, "but he wasn't exactly a star, was he?" Distancing had begun, even from a victim of a street crime.

Only in Winnie Stanfield's inner office was word of Griffin's murder received like the forerunner of disaster that it could indeed prove to be; but as such, only by Stanfield himself. He had heard it on his car radio during the inbound struggle this morning.

His secretary hadn't said anything about it until Stanfield himself muttered, "Dreadful thing about Mr. Griffin."

"Oh, Mr. Stanfield! I'm so sorry. He was such a considerate man." Her pudgy face contorted.

"I'm afraid it's incumbent on us to contact the next of kin—an elderly sister in Massachusetts, the radio report said—and offer assistance with the arrangements. Would you look into that, please?"

He moved on to his own office and shut the door behind him. A little shocking how little he knew about the man's private life. Hadn't known he'd had a sister. Forgotten he'd had a dog. The radio news story had been particularly fascinated with the dog.

Stanfield walked to his window, hands clasped behind his back, and stared down into the snow-snarled traffic on C Street. Driving in had been a bitch this morning.

. . . A Chevy Chase mugging, of all ways to exit. Death of a nervous man. Griffin *had* been jumpy when he'd left here yesterday with Swift Sword's quarter million. But wouldn't that have made anybody a trifle anxious?

Stanfield ran an abruptly trembling hand across his perfectly coiffed hair and left it rumpled. Hell, he was nervous himself.

Had Griffin delivered the money?

A disturbing scenario began to intrude on the trust in Griffin with which Stanfield was trying to reassure himself. The man takes the money, but not to Hammermill. To California? Was *that* why Griffin had for all intents given his notice yesterday? Had he been hurrying outbound when the man with the knife happened to burst from the shadows on Delaware Avenue?

Hammermill had made commitments. If the promised financial backing hadn't been delivered—Sweet Jesus!

The office temperature was comfortably regulated, but Stanfield felt a wash of sticky heat. What in hell should he do? What *could* he do at this point?

He forced himself to think . . . *think*. Did Hammermill know he was in this at all? Griffin had been an

173

honorable, devoted man. Hadn't he? It couldn't be possible that he would have revealed Stanfield's identity to Hammermill—and stolen the money. Could it?

Stanfield was trapped. He could contact the man directly. But surely Hammermill wouldn't respond to an anonymous contact. He would have to give his name. Yet, if Stanfield identified himself, then the purpose of using Griffin as an intermediary would be blown sky high.

He was hung by the balls. Not a damned thing he could do but sweat. He'd already begun to do that.

He did a lot more of it just before noon when his secretary told him a Mr. Swift was on the line. Mr. Swift? Damned coincidental, or was it?

"I'll take it, Mrs. Eames." He punched the lighted button. "Stanfield."

"Is this a secure line?" The man's voice was hard and precise.

"Secure enough."

"Secure enough is not secure enough. Find a pay phone. Call me back." The precise voice gave him a number.

Stanfield's legs were unsteady, or was it the damned snow, mashed slippery on the Virginia Avenue sidewalk? The pay phone was a chilly block away, one of those cursed wall niches in a parking garage.

"Secure now. Who in hell is this?"

"Hammermill, Mr. Stanfield."

A cold wave broke across his shoulders. "That damned Griffin—"

"You underestimate me. Griffin didn't finger you, but I think he fingered me. He was coming unglued yesterday. He said he was getting out, and I had a visit from a reporter from some New York tabloid. A little too much of a timing coincidence there for me."

"Who was the reporter?"

"Somebody named Forrest. Daniel Forrest. You know him? Stanfield, do you know him?"

The under secretary's mouth had dried. "He . . . tried to interview me Monday. I had Griffin put him off."

"He put him on, I'd say. On to me."

Stanfield was close to unable to push his next words out. "Did you get— Did Griffin deliver the—"

"Griffin delivered, yes. I'm moving ahead as planned. With my own people, Stanfield. I don't want any more Griffins."

Stanfield said nothing.

"You understand me?"

"There's no need, anyway, at this point. I'm out from here on. As planned." He understood Hammermill, all right. He understood that Dudley Griffin's murderer had been no casual street thief. "You never heard of me or Griffin, do *you* understand?" He was talking into a dead phone.

Bowlder called him in at 2:10. Up to then, this had been a rotten day. His lunch of vinaigrette salad and flounder, eaten too fast up on G Street, was boiling behind his breastbone. He'd needed the walk, but not the indigestion. Maybe the unscheduled meeting with Bowlder would force him back to business and out of the coiled spring steel of Swift Sword.

In the chief's paneled and beflagged office, the meeting began reassuringly, even with coffee in Bowlder's departmental-sealed china. Stanfield waited for others to join them and wondered with mild curiosity what this impromptu summons from the secretary of state could be about. Nicaragua's endless irritant or perhaps the new flare-up in Sri Lanka?

Bowlder placed his cup and saucer on the conference table with exaggerated precision and settled back in his chair with his hands folded across his flat belly.

"Most unfortunate, the Griffin incident."

"God, yes. I'll miss that man."

"Walking his dog, I understand."

"The dog will miss him, too. He was devoted to her." Did that sound convincing?

Bowlder's steel eyes never left Stanfield's face. "What was your aide's connection to *Red Alert,* Winnie?"

The question came at him like a spear. Stanfield realized with a mind-whirling jolt that there were to be no others at this meeting. *He* was its subject. Sour bile rose in his throat. He swallowed, and it burned.

"Red Alert?"

"That second-rate right-wing newsletter published over in Wheaton, I believe, by some nonentity named Hammermill. I had Davis Rylander do a little checking this morning."

Stanfield concentrated on keeping his voice even and disinterested. Bowlder's comment had hit him like a solid blow. "Why would Griffin have been interested in something like *Red Alert?"*

"That is the question, but I'm asking it of you. I'm asking because the Montgomery County Police searched his apartment, found Hammermill's number in Griffin's effects, and notified State Department security."

"A search like that because of a mugging?" Stanfield realized his fingers were drumming the bottom of his saucer. He put it down on the table and folded his arms. "Why would they do that?"

"At State Department security's request. Griffin was one of ours, and policy requires that now."

"I wasn't aware of that policy."

176

"Not everyone is. Did you know he had that apparent connection with *Red Alert?*"

Stanfield hesitated. Bowlder's thin, pale lips were set in an unrelenting razor slash. "No, I—"

"The truth, Winnie."

He had hesitated too long. Surely Bowlder could see the moisture beads on his upper lip. Stanfield had relished battering witnesses in Baltimore courts. Now he foresaw the first stages of such a battering about to be inflicted on himself. He didn't like it at all.

"The truth is. . . . The truth is I had no idea—"

"You are lying, Winnie." The Boston Brahmin was beginning to slice the Baltimore scrapper apart. A fingertip here, an earlobe there. Stanfield couldn't shake free of the paralysis of guilt that kept him from parrying Bowlder's attack.

"What is it, Winnie? What is going on in my own department that you can't tell me about? I realize you've had a recent personal crisis in your daughter's cruel misfortune, surely a lot for any family to bear, but especially difficult for a father alone."

Without warning, Winnie Stanfield's throat constricted. He swallowed hard, blinked, but he was pathetically unable to force back the tears. He buried his face in his hands and sobbed.

Bowlder stood abruptly, paced to the far side of the big office, studied the skyline beyond his bank of windows, returned in silence, and poured coffee for them both.

"All right." He seated himself again, crossed his legs comfortably, and rested his coffee cup and saucer on his knee. "Let me hear it."

Stanfield flooded him with a torrent of confession. Twice Bowlder asked him to slow down, take a breath, begin again. Once started, Winnie Stanfield couldn't stop,

177

not until he had blurted out the relationship with Marguerite, the intricate amassing of the quarter million, and Myra's, oh, God, Myra's—

"Slow and easy, Winnie. Slow and easy." Bowlder's voice was like that of a priest at confessional: dispassionate, unshockable, and implying succor from the basest of transgressions.

When Stanfield ultimately fell to gasping abject silence, Bowlder stared into his devastated eyes. He said, very quietly, "Oh, shit." He didn't sound like a priest then.

He didn't sound like a priest when he strode to his desk and buzzed Rylander's secretary. "I want him up here, immediately!"

"I must have been crazy," Stanfield offered in the deadly silence of the wait.

"Temporary insanity? That might wash, but I have a larger concern."

Rylander clumped in, today wearing muted gray and blue plaid with a mustard vest. He looked a lot less like a salesman as Bowlder briefed him with remarkable conciseness. What had seemed like an endlessly convoluted story when Stanfield had sobbed it to Bowlder now came off as a much neater arrangement for revenge.

Rylander pulled out his pipe. "Damage control." He glanced at Bowlder. "Sorry," he muttered and began to stuff the pipe back in his suitcoat pocket.

"Go ahead and smoke the damned thing." Bowlder shook his head slowly, then suddenly slapped the polished top of the conference table. "Damn! Remember what the White House spokesman—what was his name?—Speakes?—Remember what he once said? 'If it's something really big, the President would say it. If it was semi-big, I'd say something. If it was teeny-tiny, we'd give out a piece of paper. And if it was teeny-tinier than that, we'd let the State Department do it.' What do you think the White House would say if we announced *this*?"

"Damage control," Rylander offered again. "How many people know about this?"

Stanfield by now had had time to get something of a better hold on himself. "Besides the three of us, there's only Hammermill and whoever he's using, now that Griffin's . . . gone." He decided not to mention the reporters. What Hammermill had told him about them had been highly inconclusive anyway.

"And Hammermill's going ahead with it?"

"He has the money."

"Christ, Stanfield. A quarter mil!" Rylander shook his head in wonder. "What I couldn't do with a quarter mil. You think Hammermill's a solid enough security risk? You dead sure nobody else could have even a vague inkling of. . . . What the hell did you call it? Swift Sword?"

Stanfield hesitated again. God, what was the use now? "Hammermill did mention something about that reporter from New York who was here at the beginning of the week." And he gave up even that last bit of secrecy, the hearsay of Hammermill's encounter with Forrest.

Rylander puffed thoughtfully. "Hammermill told you that Forrest had been to see him? How the hell did Forrest work that out?"

"Maybe by way of Griffin," Stanfield guessed. "Maybe Griffin went to him or called him after Forrest was stonewalled here."

"I can't conceive of any scenario that would induce Griffin to do a thing like that, but however Forrest got to Hammermill, he's a potential link back to you, Winnie." Rylander cupped his hand around the sizzling pipe bowl,

179

took the thing out of his mouth, and contemplated its smoke tendrils. "Yet, if Griffin had told him anything concrete, you can bet your ass Forrest and his chunky assistant would have been right back here like two buzzards scenting carrion. Don't you agree?"

"You have the press expertise, Davis," Bowlder interjected gently. "What do you think?"

Rylander scowled at his pipe. "I think we go on record as denying everything that may come up about this. That'll leave Forrest with only Hammermill to build on, if he got anything out of the man at all. Let him hang Hammermill, while we blank verse him. Simple as that."

Bowlder's piercing glare swung from Rylander's face to Stanfield's. Then he offered a tight little smile that was as cold as the air outside. "I agree."

Stanfield felt a surge of relief. The lynching party had just set down its rope.

"In point of fact," Bowlder added, "if luck holds, Winnie's misbegotten Swift Sword may prove to be of benefit to us."

Rylander took out his pipe again. "Benefit?"

"Remember what one of my predecessors—I believe it was George Shultz—once said: 'There are many things that need to be done in secret.'"

Hammermill did not feel the confidence he had projected over the phone to Stanfield. Finding your office rifled didn't build confidence; a break-in shook it. But Hammermill did what he could to settle down his staff. Then he shut his office door to check his own possible losses. Gladwyn had been her predictably hysterical self. Franky hadn't said much, but her eyes showed enough distress to obviate her silence. Earl, he thought, was a touch too stoic. Might pay to keep a closer eye on Earl.

180

Or was his occupational paranoia getting in the way of analytical judgment? The God damned building was a security sieve, but who'd be interested enough in a marginal publication like *Red Alert* to bust into its offices? Surely not for money, and certainly not for its intelligence files. *Red Alert* was put together, if anyone analyzed it, from culls and dregs. An occasional correspondent did send in something of interest—and ancillary use—but the CIA and KGB were likely to have had it first. Surely *Red Alert* hadn't been honored last night by federal interest.

Which inevitably drew Hammermill to his desk. Yes, by God! Some son of a bitch had jimmied the drawer. Or had tried to. The damage was obvious, but the lock had held. Had the guy been after specifics, or had he been routinely interested in a locked drawer?

Hammermill yanked his office door open and walked to the coffee maker near Gladwyn's desk to draw himself a plastic cupful. He took it black. She and Earl had the outer office pretty well straightened up now. He looked through the open door into Franky's reception area. She was already at work on her processor keyboard. The mess out there had been that easy to set aright?

"Anybody find anything missing?" Should he call the cops?

Nobody had. Interesting. He returned to his office. Nothing had been taken from in here either. Or had it? He yanked out his keys and unlocked the drawer. The lock worked okay.

The file box was right here, where it was supposed to be. Maybe he was stupid to keep this in the office, but carrying the file with him, or stashing it somewhere more discreet, like a safe-deposit box, would be awkward and unduly risky in the first instance; prohibitively inconvenient in the second.

181

He extracted Woodman's card and tapped its edge on the desktop. Might be smart to give him a prod; keep him on track. Hammermill punched his outside line button, then fingered in Woodman's number.

The man's voice was querulous, like that of a geriatric. Some odd voice for a guy well over six feet who looked like a retired baseball pitcher and wore an athlete's indelible windburn on his flat cheeks.

"The project is on track," Woodman assured him. "You opted to leave the recruiting to me, remember? I've got a three-man team on alert in Monrovia and a Zodiac C-4 deflated in a peanut plantation warehouse, four miles up a navigable river less than twenty miles from the Nandian border. Now it's just a matter of time and timing."

Swift Sword was running on its own now. Hammermill was out of it; except for the eventual disbursement of the balance of the funding, minus, of course, his override. The transfer would be simple enough: another visit to his safe-deposit box in Bethesda, then a brief meet in the parking lot of the Marriott, Crystal City, or Holiday Inn, Key Bridge, for the car-to-car cash transfer to Woodman.

No problem with that. Hammermill hung up the phone reassured concerning the logistics. But he was no less concerned about the damned break-in.

Look at it objectively, he urged himself. Falconer had been a risk, minimal, but he'd had her taken out to obviate even her remote disintegrity potential. Griffin, potentially a far greater threat to Swift Sword's self-containment, had necessitated elimination even more emphatically. That should have terminated all nearside jeopardy. Except for Forrest, that damned persistent reporter. How much of a risk was he?

Hammermill closed the file box and slid the drawer shut. When he locked it, he noticed how little of the bolt engaged the slot in the crosspiece above, itself bent upwards slightly by the attempt to jimmy the drawer. It wouldn't have taken much to open the drawer without unlocking it.

He tried it with his letter opener. The drawer popped open with the lock's steel tongue still in place. He even got it closed again without the need to use his key.

Son of a. . . . Think, Alex Mahool. Think!

Forrest visits *Red Alert* openly, mentions Falconer and Stanfield. Then, so Gladwyn reported, he goes out to lunch with Franky. After dark, the same day, the office is broken into, the desk rifled, the drawer possibly jimmied. And the file box—

Jesus! Now he knew he wouldn't call the cops.

He didn't know where Thorp was, so he had to wait. Not an easy thing to do at this point in time. He found himself unable to concentrate on a damned thing, except the apparent new threat—an extra-operation one this time. A danger of project penetration from the outside. From a reporter he knew now he had seriously misjudged.

The man finally checked in at sixteen minutes past eight.

"It's done."

"So I heard. You still in the area?"

"Yes." Thorp's voice was as toneless as that of an orally-enhanced computer.

Hammermill drew a long breath that shook a little at the top. He hoped Thorp hadn't picked that up over the line. "I need you again," Hammermill said.

❈   ❈   ❈

Dan awoke too early. The room was dark, but flat gray had begun to outline the window's musty drapes. Dawn was working its way across Washington. He lay on his back, head cradled in his interlaced fingers, and stared up at the uneven stuccoing of the ceiling.

He had gone over and over the thing, not sleeping at all, it seemed. What disturbed him— Disturbed? What scared the hell out of him wasn't that the facts didn't fit. What did it was that, finally, sometime during the night's dark tossings, they *did* fall into place. And he knew he hadn't slept at all after that.

He had the story. Circumstantial, all of it, but he had put it together now; put together the only way the pieces could interact and make sense. What that gave him was more than a *NewsLeak* scoop. It gave him a problem: a story of conspiracy—hell, a national security matter—with no hard corroboration.

With dawn creeping around the window edges, he didn't try again to force sleep. He groaned in resignation, swung out of bed, dressed in slacks, shirt, and shoes without socks, and took the creaky elevator down for coffee, unshaven and haggard. When he returned to the room, he rapped on the connecting door. Time: 6:45.

"Coffee's on, and I've figured out what we've got."

"Okay, okay." Her voice was muzzy with interrupted sleep. "Give me a couple of minutes."

She came in promptly, despite the protest, tented in her blue robe, eyes squinty, hair minimally combed. He handed her one of the covered foam plastic cups.

"God, Daniel, you look like death barely microwaved. What's hit you?"

"Try this. Falconer is killed because she knows something she shouldn't. Griffin is killed because he knows something he shouldn't. The common denominator is Stanfield. She slept with him; Griffin was his aide."

She sat on the edge of the rumpled bed and pried the top off her coffee. "All right so far, but nothing new so far, either."

"Griffin is liaison between Stanfield and Hammermill. Stanfield's daughter has been maimed by Sokolo terrorists. Hammermill is a contractor of sorts with access to a lot of specialists."

"The green box." She was much wider awake now.

"The green box. Now why would Stanfield be doing business with a man of Mr. Hammermill-Mahool's particular talents?"

She took a pull at the coffee, eyes intent on his. "Are you saying, Daniel, that Stanfield has arranged a hit on President Sokolo?"

"That's what I'm saying."

"My God!"

"The problem is that's what *I'm* saying. We don't have any proof. It all fits, but it's all speculation."

"So where do we go from here?"

"Back to the State Department, Cork. We're going to hit them with it."

"You do have a thing for brick walls, don't you?" She drained the last of the rank coffee and set the cup down on the night table with a hard clop. "Okay," she said, looking up at him. "My head's just as hard as yours. I'll get dressed."

He made the call shortly before nine. Rylander was available, but not Stanfield. Uh-huh.

"Is he out of town?"

"He's not available."

"Mr. Rylander, this has to do with Marguerite Falconer's death, Dudley Griffin's death, and a certain Mr. Hammermill in Wheaton."

185

There was a pause at Rylander's end, only a slight one, but Dan found it significant. Then Rylander said, "I'm sorry, Mr. Forrest, we have no comment on that."

"Stonewalled again," Dan told Corkie as he hung up. "The Washington cop-out."

"It works fine, though, doesn't it? Now what?"

"Now I'd say we're desperate, and that calls for desperate tactics. I'm going to play a wild card." He leafed through his notebook, found the number he was looking for, and dialed again.

"Who—?"

He silenced her with an upraised palm. "Mr. Woodman, please."

"Daniel!"

The voice on the line was oddly quavery. And guarded. "Woodman here. Who is this?"

"Earl Rice, sir, an associate of Mr. Hammermill's here at *Red Alert*. He asked me to check on Swift Sword's progress." God forbid that Woodman had had occasion ever to talk with Rice and that Rice had a highly recognizable voice. This was already one hell of a long shot, hanging on the code name thread. Woodman was hesitating. Dan felt a ripple of apprehension.

Then Woodman said, his voice high and testy, "I gave him that information less than an hour ago."

"I know you did," Dan said smoothly, "but he's got a lot on his mind. One of the details, the number of men . . ." Come on, Woodman, come on. I'm running out of ingenious ideas.

Another hesitation. Woodman cleared his throat with a peculiar whinnying sound. "A three-man squad, damn it, by Zodiac boat to the Nandian Coast, as soon as Sokolo's schedule is confirmed. Tell him to *listen* next time, Rice."

186

"Daniel," Corkie said with a grin as he replaced the receiver, "that was not at all ethical."

"Neither is assassination. We got it, Cork!" He tossed his empty cup in the air and slapped it toward the wastebasket. "Hammermill has contracted a hit on Sokolo!"

"We got enough to file a story on?"

"If it's put together right."

She walked to the window and gazed into the snow-covered parking area, now rutted with icy tire tracks. The Chevette was shrouded in a pearly crust, as were the scattered cars still in place. Except for one that pulled in beside the Chevette while she watched—a gunmetal blue—something. She didn't know the make, but it looked expensive. It was clean and shiny, a sleek new arrival with New York plates, out of context at this down-at-the-heels stopover.

"Should we?" she asked as she turned away from the window.

"What do you mean, should we?"

"Sokolo is an international murderer. Wouldn't we all be better off without him?"

"You're saying we should stay out of it? Let the thing go ahead?"

"It's a thought."

"It's Stanfield's and Hammermill's thought, and it's already killed two people. One of them, in all probability, was an innocent bystander. Our side is just as ruthless as the other side."

"Our side?"

"Well, this side."

"But heading the thing off won't save Marguerite Falconer and Dudley Griffin. They're already gone, Daniel. Putting Sokolo out of the way would save a lot of future anguish. Agreed?"

187

"I'm a newspaper man, Corkie, not an international strategist. Leave that up to the State Department."

"That's exactly what I'm suggesting we seriously think about."

"Oh, nicely put. But Stanfield isn't the whole State Department. We're going higher. We're going over there and camp on the doorstep until we get through."

"You're sure?"

"Yeah, I'm sure. I'm after a story."

They didn't get there.

The timing had made tracking down Forrest seem more difficult than it actually was. Hammermill hadn't had the foresight to ask the guy where he was staying, which would have been most helpful to Thorp.

"No phone number? Nothing?" Thorp had pushed, when the contract had been set during the phone call to Hammermill this morning just after eight.

"Sorry. I just wanted to get rid of the guy."

"What was his paper's name?"

That Hammermill had been able to give him. Thorp had a name and a place of employment. Information had given him a number.

No answer in New York. He waited fifteen minutes; tried again. The time now was 8:34. Five rings; then it was picked up.

"*NewsLeak.* Jonathan Blauvelt here."

"I'd like to speak with Daniel Forrest?"

"Not here. Sorry."

"Will he be in this morning?"

"Afraid not. He's in Washington on assignment."

"I have information that concerns that assignment, Mr. Blauvelt. Do you know where he is staying?"

And Blauvelt, all innocent helpfulness, knew. Thorp left the Sheraton Inn Washington-Northwest at 8:50,

188

hoping Forrest was a slow starter. He pulled into the Largo motel parking lot a few minutes after nine. One New York car, but he wasn't sure whether the man had driven or flown or taken Amtrak and rented a local car.

Course of action? He would wait a reasonable time for the New York registration to come out of the place. After that, he was going to have to take the risk of an appearance at the desk to get Forrest's room number. Or, better yet, he could call the desk from the pay phone across Route 214 in the service station's—

Then, in his side mirror, he saw a couple step out of the motel entrance: a middle-aged guy with thinning light-colored hair in a beat-up raincoat, and a heavy woman in a dark-colored wool tent. Hammermill hadn't said anything about a woman, but the guy fit his description of Forrest. And they were headed straight for the tan Chevette.

Two of them . . . if this was Forrest. How was he going to handle two of them? His plan to invite Forrest into the Mazda with the inducement of the Safari Enforcer held close to his body was unraveling fast. He had intended to drive Forrest into rural Maryland and leave him out there, none too neatly holed, caliber .45. Certainly not as slick an execution as Griffin's, nor as deceptive as Falconer's. But Hammermill wanted this done fast. Today. Now.

And it came to him. It could be neat, after all. An accident in the Chevette on a slippery country road. Thorp slid out of the RX-7.

"Mr. Forrest? Are you Daniel Forrest?"

The man looked at him over the Chevette's roof and paused in his windshield cleaning.

Standing between the cars, beside the woman, Thorp had the automatic in his right hand. He grabbed her arm with his left and shoved the gun's muzzle in her ribs.

"Dan!" she squealed. "He has a gun!"

"Keep it down, keep it down," Thorp ordered. "Forrest, you get in the Chevette and follow us. Don't lose me, you hear, or you lose her. Get in," he told the woman. "Crawl over the console and get in the passenger seat."

For a big broad, she did that pretty well. He followed her rump in and held the gun on her with his left hand. It would make a hell of a racket in here, maybe even bust an eardrum; but the way she looked now, all white and guppy-mouthed, he figured he wouldn't have to use it.

A good thing, too. Driving with one hand and holding the Enforcer on her with the other was damned awkward. Maybe he should have made her drive, but nobody handled this baby but him.

He pulled onto Route 214's newly scraped pavement and headed for the Capital Beltway. In the rearview, the Chevette fell into place fifty feet behind. Not a bad plan, considering the few seconds he'd had to come up with it. Not bad at all. With fat girl here as hostage, Forrest would stick glue-tight wherever Thorp wanted to take them.

Word had come in the darkness; whispered word through the barely opened door on the third floor of the stifling Monrovia hotel. A bit of a far cry from his native Sydney this muggy city was, Aussie Harkness thought, as his informant padded off into the corridor's fetid silence. At least, it was a far cry from the Sydney he remembered. He hadn't been down under since he had dusted off to fight Lumumba. There had been some money in that. More in Angola, a mercenary's gourmet

190

menu. Left side, right side, the money still hadn't run out.

War to war he'd lived. And almost died more than once. The Claymore mine just outside Benguela. Poor cobber beside him had taken most of it. Unlucky for him; lucky for Harkness. The stray Kalashnikov round in Nova Lisboa. Just about spent when it smacked him in the shoulder, but it had enough wallop to knock him clear out of the Land Rover. A half-inch lower, and it would have pinked the subclavian artery. And them not within twenty miles of an aid squad. Luck of the game. He'd gotten past forty with no more than nicks and bruises, and that one puncture that had left a puckered scar the size of a Yank quarter. American was the currency he preferred to deal in; they all did.

Harkness was only superficially scarred physically. Mentally he'd had it with taking orders from homegrown, overfed colonels, a mile out of their depth, while the savvy mercs and poor sucker patriots bled and died for officers' errors. *That* was the real risk: the ever-ominous threat that some dumb-as-muck Angolan or Sudanese or Libyan ranker would order his mercs into the most elementary of ambushes.

Which was why Harkness had become a specialist, an independent contractor for precisely the kind of mission that was now laid on, thanks to the whispered confirmation from his liaison wog in the corridor. The assignments came from Chapelle in the south of France, from Landermann in Haifa, from Woodman in the States.

This one was from Woodman, which was a bit of all right, since Woodman paid promptly, and in American. He'd already transmitted the money for the boat and the two Ghanaians Harkness had subcontracted for the mission. They were good men, he felt, one of whom he'd worked with before. They had slipped into Liberia

191

a week ago and waited in a safe house in Monrovia's raggedy outskirts.

He picked them up at 2:55 A.M., and the three of them set off northwest for the obscure Boporu River. Harkness drove a vintage U.S. Army Jeep he had bought for a song from a near-bankrupt Monrovia-based tour company. No rich Americans wanted to see the wonders of West Africa now. Sokolo had seen to that.

They reached the river at dawn, the Jeep's howling engine and high-load gearing drowning the psittacine shrieks and monkey yowls along the overgrown river-bank. The road, now narrow dirt hardpan, paralleled the sluggish waterway, which they occasionally glimpsed through breaks in the mangroves. Every mile they bounced the Jeep upriver now meant another mile of retracing by water along essentially the same route.

The larger of the pair of Ghanaians had accompanied Harkness on an extended trek into Mali and a quick kill along the Niger, just east of Bamako. Damongo, his name was. Harkness recalled him as a man of grunts, though he did have a fair grip on basic English. His previous association with Harkness merited him the front passenger seat of the Jeep.

Both the Ghanaians had the near-Caucasian features of many North African blacks, and both wore loose uniforms of surplus British regulation khaki shorts and short-sleeved khaki shirts, contrasting with Harkness's gray cotton duck slacks and long-sleeved tan shirt. He wasn't at all partial to sun. His headgear was a battered Aussie bush hat that threw his flattish face, stubby nose, and squinty close-set blue eyes in deep shadow. The Ghanaians were bareheaded.

The two blacks dressed the same and had the same chiseled features, but there the similarity ended. The stiffly erect Damongo in the front seat beside Harkness

192

had an aura of military training and experience. He had been, in fact, one of the garrison sergeants who had not assisted in barring President Nkrumah from his own palace when that ill-fated luminary had returned from a trip out of the country to find the locks had been changed on the palace doors. Sergeant Damongo had found it prudent shortly thereafter to desert, ultimately to leave the country. Now he existed—sometimes thrived—on the fees from short-term special assignments for custom-work mercs like Aussie Harkness.

The man jolting listlessly in the back seat, Yendi by name and a willing murderer by reputation, had enjoyed no military background. He was jail bred, a product of a seven-year term for a knife killing during a drunken brawl in Accra, followed by another four years for street robbery after his release. During the second term, he had acquired the nasty razor slash down the left side of his face, from forehead to earlobe, a souvenir of inmate bickering that had left him with a sardonic droop of the left eye, where its outer corner had been nicked by the descending blade.

When he'd gotten out the second time, he had determined that he would never again go in for petty crime. He slipped across the Ivory Coast border into Liberia, and it didn't take him long to become available to the little groups of hard men who frequently and quietly disappeared from Monrovia to return days or weeks later, their eyes glittering with accomplishment and their pockets newly lined with money. Harkness had hired Yendi on Damongo's recommendation, but since he had not yet worked with either man, Yendi knew he was being tested on this trip. He had one advantage over them. He knew the Nandian Coast. They did not.

The sun was well above the mangroves when the Jeep reached the corrugated metal warehouse at the south edge of the plantation. The agreement with the mulatto overseer centered on neglect. For the Liberian dollars he had already received, he had neglected to concern himself with the tarpaulin-covered bundles in the warehouse's dim southeast corner. He would also fail to notice the three men soon to be hard at work in there and on the adjacent dock, and he would not hear the muttered pock-pock of the hand-operated pneumatic pump.

The preparations took just over thirty-seven minutes, and, in all that time, not a single plantation hand appeared. Most of the riverside preparation period was taken by the wait for Damongo to inflate the bouyancy tubes of the Zodiac C-4 Commando with the stubby gray plastic pump. Some of that wait was gainfully used by Harkness to field-strip and wipe clean the three blocky Ingram M-10s. The weapon was not a familiar one to Yendi. Harkness checked him out as best he could with dry-firing. The important factors were to know how to load, cock, and trigger it. Aiming wasn't critical. With its multiple-burst 1,090-rounds-per-minute cycling rate, one could hardly miss putting some of a 32-round magazine where it was supposed to go.

When the black Plastomer-coated fabric boat was inflated sausage-tight, they stored the guns and ammo beneath a tarp amidships on the aluminum decking. Harkness and Damongo clamped the 40-horse Evinrude on the plywood transom, filled its fuel tank from one of the five-gallon cans they had brought aboard. Fuel consumption was critical. The Evinrude had a six-gallon capacity and burned up about a gallon every five miles. The smaller Ghanaian had shown Harkness on his map that their destination was some one hundred thirty miles distant. After their bit of business, Harkness would put himself and his two freelancers ashore at least fifty miles west of the execution site. They would split up and make their separate ways from there. Harkness intended to return to Monrovia. He didn't know or care about the other two.

Overall distance: one hundred eighty statute miles, plus or minus a minor error factor. At six gallons per tank filling, times five nominal miles per gallon, each tankful would drive them thirty miles. That meant five refuellings, thirty-six gallons in all. Harkness had arranged for eight cans, one now empty and the remaining seven stored on the floorboard. That gave them a four-gallon margin of safety. The boat was crowded, but as each can was emptied, it would be jettisoned, and one normally rode a Zodiac sitting on the buoyancy tubes anyway.

They would leave behind, in addition to the Zodiac's and the engine's containers, only the Jeep. That was acceptable because the Jeep was part of the overseer's payment. If asked, he was sworn to say he had bought it in Monrovia with two years of savings.

At ten minutes after nine, Aussie Harkness motioned his men aboard, stepped from the rickety wooden dock into the Zodiac's stern, and, with one of the emergency paddles, shoved the fourteen-foot inflatable into the Boporu's slow current. The river was some three hundred feet wide here, a broad, coffee-colored drift sliding endlessly toward the coast.

With the paddle, Harkness manhandled the laden boat close to the shoreline trees, staying in their deep shadow, until the current had carried the boat and its three occupants more than a mile downriver.

The outboard engine, a relatively new one, started on the second pull of the lanyard. Harkness held it on idle for another quarter mile. Then he twisted the throttle control up to planing speed.

The Zodiac's blunt prow lifted. The propeller dug in astern. Then the assault boat leveled off high in the water. The assassination team thrummed toward the river mouth and the open Atlantic at a steady fifteen knots.

12

THERE HAD BEEN very few times since he'd sworn off the stuff that Dan had felt totally helpless. This surely was one of them.

The son of a bitch in the Mazda had him good. Thorp—odds were excellent that the guy was the *spec. in elmntn.* in Hammermill's card file—really had him nailed. Dan was in his control as inexorably as if he had the muzzle of Thorp's automatic shoved under his own ribs. Hell, Dan was under even tighter control than that. If he were in the Mazda with Thorp, he might have been able to work out something positive—ram a foot on the brake, grab the gun. Who knew? But with Corkie up there and himself back here trailing along ineffectually in the Chevette, that wasn't an option.

He followed the sports coupe's blunt rear up the access ramp to the Capital Beltway and eased into the morning traffic, careful to hold his fifty-foot distance behind.

What the hell *were* his options? One obvious one, of course. Just go with the flow and see what happens.

197

Not a happy outlook, that one; not with Thorp's performance rating to date. Pretty damned obvious now who had killed Marguerite Falconer. And the odds that Dudley Griffin had fatally met a common street mugger were zilch. Thorp, Hammermill's *spec. in elmntn.*, was systematically doing his work, closing off loopholes.

Dan smacked the steering wheel with a frustrated fist. *Jesus!* This was a hell of a thing! He had the story, had guessed right every step of the way, knew who was doing what and to whom. Yet he couldn't prove it, and now he couldn't do a damned thing about it.

Or could he?

Drive erratically and hope to be picked up by a state or county cop? Then what? What cop would believe a nutso story like the one he'd have to tell? While he told it, the Mazda would be long gone. Dan could provide description and license number, but there was no guarantee that Thorp wouldn't promptly switch plates—or even cars—and leave Corkie alone on a deserted side road with a bullet in her.

Cut out and find a phone? Same potential outcome.

He wasn't a free agent, not with her and Thorp and the gun in the car ahead. The guy had looked like a colorless librarian, until Dan had stared hard into his eyes. No color there, either, but the pale gray irises had been cold as this January morning. There had been a message in those pale eyes. It told him that Thorp had put a price on their lives, and he had been guaranteed payment.

Another option: ram the Mazda, force it off the road, and take his chances after that. The problem would be that he'd be forcing Corkie to take her chances along with him. Not good. The only practical option was to comply and wait for, hope for, opportunity. Hell of a choice.

198

The Mazda's turning signal began to blink well in advance of Exit 35. Dan trailed the steel blue RX-7 down the ramp into 270, bound northwest. In less than fifteen minutes, they were well out of urban sprawl, cutting through snow-blanketed hills on the divided highway.

West of Little Bennett Regional Park, Thorp swung off the interstate into a fishhook exit ramp to double back beneath the highway. Dan followed the Mazda west on a rural road that had been plowed down to hardpan snow.

He had thought of Maryland as a fairly flat state, when he'd thought of it at all. But that was because he'd traveled only its eastern and central areas. Here, northwest of Washington, the land was broken by steepening hills.

At a remote crossroad, the Mazda swung right into a narrower, snow-rutted roadway. Three miles on, they thundered over a rickety wooden bridge that spanned a broad, iced-over creek. Then they climbed and dipped through increasingly hilly countryside. At last, in the hills south of Frederick, Thorp apparently found what he was so desperately looking for. He pulled over and stopped on the crest of an abrupt rise. Dan put the Chevette on the shoulder a good hundred feet behind. Now what?

Thorp got out, stood beside his car with his coat flapping in the wind. He aimed the automatic through the window straight at Corkie's head and, with his free hand, motioned to Dan.

Dan moved the Chevette forward obediently, but he was seething inside. Would it be possible to run the bastard down where he stood? Catch him with the Chevette's right front fender and flip him neatly and fatally over the Mazda's hood—or jam him between the two cars?

If the pistol had been aimed at him, instead of at Corkie, Dan might have tried that. But what would happen in the split second of contact when Thorp's finger tendons clamped in uncontrollable reaction?

Dan glided the Chevette to a stop beside the Mazda, with Thorp between the two cars. He reached across the seat and rolled down the window.

"Pull off the shoulder just ahead, front of the car to the edge of the bank."

Beyond Thorp in the Mazda, Dan could see Corkie's fear-drained face imploring him to . . . do something. If he was scared, she had to be close to panic after riding more than forty miles with a gun muzzle in her side.

Do what? Pull something right now and get her killed in the next five seconds? Dan had wondered what he would do under threat of a gun, when he knew that the ultimate outcome of doing nothing would be a bullet anyway. The fast-food manager lies on the restaurant floor listening to the approaching pops, as the crazed thief head-shoots the employees one by one. Yet the manager lies there obediently, hands behind his back as ordered, hearing death come closer, shot by shot. Is his inaction a matter of disbelief? A desperate grab at a few more seconds of life?

And Marguerite Falconer apparently had stripped, let Thorp snap on handcuffs, and slip the silken rope around her neck; hadn't struggled. Was she simply hoping for a few more seconds of life, until the rope had choked off all hope?

Dan pulled ahead and to the right, as Thorp had directed. And now he knew the man's intention. The Chevette perched at the brink of a steep drop-off, a nearly straight fall into a rocky defile fifty feet below. No Grand Canyon, but more than a ton of car with two

200

people in its front seat would be slammed into scrap by the impact.

Nice, Thorp. No skid marks up here yet, but the Mazda would put them there for the accident investigators. And sure, here came Corkie at gunpoint to join him for the ride down.

What were they doing way out there, Charlie—among others—would be sure to ask. That would be part of it, the out-of-context confusion. What had Marguerite Falconer been doing with cuffs and a rope? Griffin's exit hadn't been quite as diverting, but Dan reasoned that Thorp had been rushed on that one by oncoming traffic or perhaps by another evening stroller. Or by a tightening time frame.

Not much chance of that out here. Nothing but naked trees, snow-bleached hills, and an overcast of dirty wool.

She got in the car beside him, shuddering but trying not to show it. "Dan—" Her voice was a parched squeak. He couldn't fault her for that. "We could run," she managed. "Go in different directions."

That was damned gutsy for a lady who looked as if she couldn't run worth a damn.

"He'd have us both in ten seconds. Buckle your seat belt."

Behind them, the Mazda's rotary engine ripped. The low-slung sports car pulled off the shoulder into the roadside weeds and began to close the gap between them.

From the crest of the hill, Dan checked the road ahead and back the way they'd come. Clear for the entire mile he could see each way. Where was traffic when you needed it?

He had left the Chevette's engine running. Now he slipped the gears into reverse. The space between

201

the rear bumper and the Mazda's shark nose had narrowed to twenty feet. Just a few seconds left before the far more powerful sports car made contact and irresistibly bulldozed them over the edge to plunge nosedown onto the rocks below. One tiny chance here . . .

"Get your head back!" Dan ordered. He cramped the wheel hard right, and he floored the accelerator.

The little car leaped backward, clanged into the oncoming Mazda, and slewed to a halt at the lip of the cliff. Its rear bumper hung over empty air. The car teetered. Dan shot the shift lever into drive. The wheels spun, threw twin fans of dirty snow high over the gully, caught, and he whirled the Chevette around the rear of the scrabbling Mazda.

They hit the snow-covered shoulder with a hell of a bounce, slewed wildly into the roadway. He gunned the little car out of there, heading back the way they had come.

"Beautiful!" Corkie gasped. She twisted around. "Oh, God, Dan! He's coming. And fast!"

Just great. They could have used something above Indy class, and *NewsLeak*'s budget had stuck them with a skateboard.

The Mazda caught them in less than a mile, hung behind them like a maddened blue shark waiting to strike. Waiting for what?

The damned sports car tailgated them for three miles, three miles of winding, swooping, snow- and ice-glazed rural road where they saw no one, not a stray dog or foraging rabbit, until they whistled past a pick-up truck waiting behind a stop sign at a side road. Fat lot of help that was.

Thorp's nearly bumper-to-bumper pursuit had a purpose, Dan realized. The hit man's intent was to crowd the hell out of them, to keep Dan off balance, to press

202

him into a panic, where he'd be likely to make a fatal mistake.

Two miles past the crossroad, as they neared the ramshackle little bridge they had rumbled across not more than ten minutes ago, Thorp made his move.

The onrushing bridge was one that should have been replaced years ago. Located here in sparsely populated country, though, it had been listed low priority and carried forward year after year as a matter for the next administration to handle.

All that was evident in Dan's glance at the pitted, ice-coated macadam of its road surface and the rusty bolting of its gray timber siderails. The ice-locked creek spanned by the bridge was no more than sixty feet wide, but the instant the Mazda loomed huge in the Chevette's rearview mirror, Dan knew the possibility Thorp had seen.

The man thought fast, Dan had to give him that. Thorp no doubt held his planning ability in nicely inflated self-esteem. That would be par for a successful contractor like him. A character flaw, because it would nicely help him to underestimate everyone else.

Something sure as hell made him underestimate Dan, because when he rammed the Mazda's snout hard into the Chevette's rear bumper fifty yards from the bridge, he couldn't have expected it to jink sideways clear off the road, brake hard, then squeeze back in a split second and ram sideways into him.

The little car crunched into his right door, bounced away, banged in again. At least four hundred bucks' damage, you son of a bitch!

Dan pulled free again, then he floored the accelerator and hit the Mazda at a steeper angle.

The sports car was powerful, but not heavily built. The impact jumped it sideways. Its front left tire caught an edge of the crumbling bridge approach macadam. The Mazda slewed sharply left.

Dan caught a glimpse of Thorp's white face, his mouth a black O, like an oversized bullet hole. It might as well have been a bullet hole. The Mazda's shark snout hood caught the lower horizontal timber of the bridge railing. The car's hurtling dead weight tore the timber loose from its ancient uprights. The hood's sloped configuration jacked it neatly upward.

The six-by-six butt end obliterated the windshield in a crystal explosion. The Mazda's bumper sheared off six upright posts as the horizontal rail slammed the length of the vehicle's interior. The car stopped abruptly, impaled on the unyielding thirty-foot-long six-by-six.

Thorp never had a chance.

All that took place in less than five seconds, the time Dan's eyes flicked leftwards to take in the catastrophic demolition of the left-hand bridge railing. Then he wrenched his focus back to the onrushing roadway.

The Chevette's final impact against the swerving Mazda had a continuing effect. The right side railing grew huge as the Chevette refused to respond to Dan's frantic leftward whirl of the wheel. The car's front end took out two of the bulky wooden uprights, as if they were made of balsa. The front wheels hit the railing's raised concrete footing. The Chevette bounded upwards. Its free-flying front end banged through the two brittle horizontal timbers as if they'd been hit by a giant sledge. The rear wheels smacked the footing, were deflected upwards. The Chevette soared off the side of the bridge into empty air.

Dan heard a shrill keening. Corkie's scream. He heard the engine, freed of traction load, howl wildly. His foot clamped uselessly on the brake. He smelled the sudden sweat of terror, caught a glimpse—like the flick of a camera shutter—of gray overcast, the leafless tops of trees. Then the Chevette nosed down. The snow-covered ice of the creek rushed upwards.

They hit with an explosive crash. His shoulder strap clamped a diagonal of hard pain across Dan's chest. Corkie's shrill screech cut off abruptly.

The impact left him fighting for breath. Through a confusion of chest pain and dancing dots that threatened to merge into blinding blackout, he was conscious of a series of ragged cracklings. The car began to settle.

"You all right?" he cried idiotically. His voice sounded like sandpaper on dry wood.

"The ice— Dan, we're sinking!"

And damned fast. They had hit flat, but the impact had shattered the creek's thick coating. He shoved hard on the door, but the sills were already six inches below the surface. Jagged ice edges jammed the doors solidly shut.

Water began to pour through the hinge fittings and apertures in the engine compartment's firewall; it covered their shoes and rose rapidly. The inrushing water climbed higher as the car settled. Dan's ankles, then his calves, were numbed by its frigid impact.

Thorp was dead. But he had won. They were trapped, rapidly sinking in ice water that would first rob them of mobility, then kill them with hypothermia in minutes.

Not without a fight, damn it!

"The seat belt, Corkie. Release it!"

Her terrified eyes were uncomprehending. He reached down into the rising water, hit her release and his, and grabbed her arm.

"Listen to me! When this thing goes under, we'll be able to open the doors. We can get out. When I tell you, open your door and push out of here."

She stared at him blankly. He'd seen that look on some fellow grunts in 'Nam, right after a shell hit.

With both hands, he shook her. "Damn it, we're going to get out, girl! Don't quit on me."

The water level had risen past their waists, paralyzing in its frigidity. But now his legs felt warm again. Warm? They felt nothing at all. And that was a greater danger: the urge to succumb to hypothermia's predeath anesthesia.

His teeth vibrated in the arctic water's ascending grip. "When we're un . . . under, the doors will open. Concentra . . . te on that."

God, let the creek be deep enough for the doors to sink clear of the ice.

"We're drowning!" she gasped.

"Air space. Should be air trapped—"

The swirling water swept into his mouth, cut off his words before he could take a final breath to hold. The car thudded on the creek bottom.

He reached through the numbing gray flood, felt her upper arm, gripped it, forced his other hand to seize the bunched cloth of her coat. Shoved upwards, as strength drained away.

Lungs bursting, he found air, a flat, three-inch bubble of it trapped against the shallow curve of the Chevette's roof. His clubby hands thrust her chin up out of the dark water. He heard her choke, cough. Breathe.

"Now, out!" he ordered.

She was wild-eyed, but trying. She went under again. He followed her down, forcing numb legs and arms to work, pushed around her, and found the door handle on her side. His fingers closed over hers. Together they made the damned thing work. Her legs thrust sluggishly against him as the door inched open, swirling up a brown cloud of creek-bed residue.

206

He jackknifed sideways with his feet against his door. He hoped they were; he could barely feel anything at all.

The water was dark as twilight. He could make her out only dimly as he set his shoulder against her rump and shoved with the feeble, fading strength of his legs.

She bumped through the opening. He clawed out behind her, clumsy as a drunk wearing baseball mitts. But they were out.

She began to drift upwards listlessly, much too slowly. He managed to roll over and look up. They were in ten or twelve feet of water. He could see the hole the Chevette had slammed through the translucent ice sheet, its jagged edges blurred by his underwater inability to focus. Silvery air bubbles drifted beneath the frosted surface.

Escape was only a dozen feet away, but he had nothing left, not an ounce of energy now. The merciless cold had taken it all, drained him. And he needed air. God, how he needed air! He let out a string of bubbles to fool his lungs into thinking he was about to breathe again.

Shoving up those twelve feet was impossible. A numb lassitude gripped him. Easy now to let it all go, so damned easy. Who said dying had to be hard?

Then he caught a blurry motion beside him. Corkie had thrust out an arm in what had to be a last desperate effort to get out of here. He didn't know where his final few ounces of energy came from. Maybe from seeing her still fighting, despite the constricting cold and the drag of her sodden coat and the overwhelming temptation to quit.

He forced his arm to reach out, touch her. And he found new strength. Not much of it, but enough to drift

207

them upwards together. Toward the ragged break in the ice above the submerged car. Toward air.

They broke surface. Choked. Gagged. Dragged in huge lungfuls of clean, cold oxygen. Dan managed to raise one leaden arm free of the water, but there was no feeling in it. None at all. There was no way they could climb out on the ice. His eyes unfocused. He saw only a brilliant blur as he began to slip back down.

Then a darker mass appeared in the middle of the frosty whiteness.

He squinted. The dark area slowly drew into near sharpness. A beard, a mass of wild black hair under a brown knit watch cap. Close-set eyes above a blobby nose.

The beard opened into a wide mouth. "Hey!" Dan heard fuzzily. "Hey, buddy, hang in there, God damn it!" The man lay flat on the ice, his face not a foot from Dan's. Powerful arms reached out, grabbed his shoulders.

"Get her," Dan managed through blue lips. "Get . . . Corkie—"

"Asa's got her," the big face said. Then the beard, the wild hair, the squinty eyes all merged into a mass of dancing black specks that grew, overlapped, and faded into nothing.

He felt sharp slaps on his face, on one cheek, then the other. "Don't crap out on us now! Come on, buddy!" The voice was distant. Then it came in right beside his ear, like TV volume suddenly turned up. He was hunched on the creek bank, dripping, shuddering, chattering in a red plaid jacket—the bearded man's jacket, because now the man was in woolen shirt-sleeves.

Close by, Corkie huddled in a fur-collared khaki jacket, and a second man in a plaid shirt stood over her, taller than the man with the beard, his sharper features clean shaven.

"Best thing, Monk," he was saying, "is take them over to Bushey's farm. Only 'bout a mile on. Phone the cops and an ambulance from there."

In the pickup, with Asa riding the open body to make room for them in the cab, Monk turned the heat full on. He nodded toward the impaled Mazda. "Not a damn thing we could do for him. Hell of a sight. I told Asa, when you people flew past back there, I told him, 'There's an accident just looking for a place to happen.' Sure found a hell of a place."

Dan felt pressure on his forearm. Corkie's fingers, still blue under the nails, held him in a grip of which she seemed oblivious. Her eyes, squinting against the chills that shuddered her against him, stared straight through the windshield. He wondered what she was seeing, but decided not to ask. Then his hand slid over hers. She turned to him, blinked. Smiled a little.

By the time they reached the farm, were loaned dry clothes by white-haired Evan Bushey and his much younger but no less chore-worn wife, and let the big fire in the living room dissolve what had seemed like a permanent chill, Dan and Corkie managed to head off Monk's insistence that an ambulance be called.

He finally relented. "But the state cops'll sure want to talk to you."

"Fine, but what we need most now is the use of that phone."

In the alcove beneath the farmhouse stairs, Corkie said to him, "Not the State Department again?"

"Three people have been killed, Cork, and we've been threatened at gunpoint, assaulted by a motor vehicle, and damned near drowned. I'd say the time for futzing around on this thing is over." He gave the operator the number. "Reverse the charges," he added.

209

"That'll help focus Charlie's attention," he said to Corkie.

"Dan," Charlie's voice rumbled, "what in the hell are you doing on the story, for corn sake?"

"We've got it, Charlie. Hell of a story. Dateline: *Washington.* Lead: *'Three people have died in an apparent bizarre revenge plot to assassinate President Benjamin Sokolo of the Peoples Republic of Nandia. Only through luck did two* NewsLeak *reporters escape with their lives—' "*

"Hey, whoa! Hold it!" Charlie yelped. "What are you giving me?"

"Damnedest story you ever heard, Charlie. *NewsLeak* won't be out soon enough for this one, and it sure won't keep. But you can sell a summary to AP, then give it full treatment in our next issue. They'll be wrestling over it at the checkout counters. Couple of details, Charlie. I sank the rental car."

"You *what!"*

"And—" Dan caught Corkie's eye. "And I want a double byline on this one. Daniel Forrest and Cornelia Brion. You got that, Charlie?"

"*Sank* the car?" Charlie sounded as if he were gargling with vinegar.

"Pay attention, Charlie." And Dan gave him the story.

"Don't forget AP, Charlie," he said when he wrapped it up.

"I'm thinking about it."

Not for long, though. It was on the press wires before noon. Double byline.

Davis Rylander had his hands full. The story had broken on the broadcast media at noon and in early editions of eastern evening papers not much later. Rylander's people were desperately dike-thumbing, as he put it. "Denial, denial, denial," he urged, but Jesus, talk about bailing with a sieve! He had really underestimated that damned tabloid team. The shit would roll rapidly downhill on this one.

Rylander called that right. The summons from Bowlder's office came at 1:57, the instant the chief had returned from lunch in the Senate dining room with the chairman of the Senate Foreign Relations Committee. Rylander ran into Stanfield at the head of Bowlder's office corridor. What was there to say? The man looked as if the world had deflated all over him.

So did Bowlder. The three of them stood glumly around the conference table. No one sat. No one touched the coffee. They stared at each other.

Then Bowlder blinked.

"We can minimize," he said desperately. "Get a warning to Sokolo on record. That's important. Get it on record."

"We have no diplomatic relations with Nandia."

"Through the Swiss, Stanfield. They have a legation there."

Stanfield, Bowlder had called him. Not the familiar Winnie now. The chief had no doubt already picked Stanfield's career sump—if the man somehow survived the inevitable legal fallout. Upper Volta or hooray for Allenwood, Stanfield. Either way, the man was dead meat, careerwise.

"Meantime," Bowlder said, "I want you out of here. Incommunicado even to staff. You understand that, Stanfield?"

"Yes, sir. I'll be at home."

"Have someone you trust to short-stop your phone. Davis, send one of your people with him. You'll know how to brief him."

Or her. Rylander would assign Mary Costigan to this one. She was good with innuendo. The message Rylander was getting was one of load shifting. Get as much of this off the Department and onto Stanfield.

Too bad, Rylander thought as they filed out. They had to save one of the world's bloody butchers to rescue their own butts. What kind of justice was that?

Or had they already blown it? What Stanfield called Swift Sword was already underway, he'd told them. What the hell would be the rolldown if they weren't able to get through to Sokolo in time?

13

HARKNESS HUGGED the rock cliffs of the Nandian coastline as daylight faded. The three-man team had made way several miles out to sea through the day, the Zodiac's low profile of plasticized fabric making no impact on Nandian radar, Harkness knew. The coastline offered no deepwater harbor, no defense facilities save a few coastal radar artillery emplacements. The Soviet-built installations were second-line equipment, sited for aircraft detection.

He and the big Ghanaian depended on the man with the scarred face now. He knew the coastal detail. They did not. He had promised them an accessible landing site, but Harkness had begun to wonder about that. The shoreline cliffs continued unbroken as the Evinrude muttered them along in intensifying darkness just offshore of the low-breaking surf.

The timing was right, if the taciturn Ghanaian was right. They would hit Sokolo's vacation villa at full dark.

The smaller black man riding the blunt bow raised his arm, fingers extended. Harkness throttled down. The

Zodiac nosed around a hulking promontory, its flat bottom slapping as they lost weigh. The untested Ghanaian had proved his worth. A stretch of sand became slowly visible on the far side of the steep outcrop.

Harkness guided the Zodiac to the near corner of the little beach. He cut the engine. They rode the low waves inbound, then scrubbed ashore on the secluded sand apron. They were concealed by a rock ledge from any vantage point higher ashore.

"Refuel now," Harkness ordered Damongo. "We'll be coming out of here full tilt."

The big black uncapped the last of the gas cans and began to empty it into the Evinrude's tank. The fuel consumption had exceeded Harkness's estimate, but these last six gallons would get them at least thirty miles distant after the coming dust-up. Aussie Harkness and Yendi unshipped the Ingrams, loaded them, and set aside two additional magazines for each man to stuff inside his shirt.

When the refueling was completed, the three of them moved single file around the shielding jut of rock, Harkness in the lead. They moved upwards slowly, close by the sharp rock shoulder left by Sokolo's contractor, when his crew had blasted and scraped this hundred yards of shoreline smooth enough to receive one thousand tons of imported sand to create Sokolo's private beach.

The sand sloped gradually upwards, then dwindled away against a pebbly continuation of the rise. At its crest, five hundred feet from the water's edge, Harkness saw the glimmer of lights in the loom of a building. The presidential villa hunkered up there, low and black against the night's starless gray. Behind it, he could make out the silhouette fringe of palms.

At his direction, they avoided the flagstone walkway that ascended the center of the graveled portion of the hillside and kept well to the right. The shelter of the beach's shoulder fell below them. Now Harkness felt exposed, though there was no sign of a sentry, dogs, alarm trips; nothing but the sibilant wash of the waves behind them. With the beach as background, he hoped their light-colored clothing would help obscure their approach, were anyone in the villa glancing seaward. Harkness also hoped his unconfirmed information on Sokolo's vacation security arrangements was accurate. It had been reported to be casual at best out here in what could be considered Nandia's own Outback.

The villa was a seventy- or eighty-foot masonry ramble across the brow of the hill. A darkened veranda ran its full width. Harkness's team crossed its warm flagstones. A shoe scraped. They froze.

There was no response from behind the lighted central window nor the two illuminated rectangles at the left side, which Harkness presumed to be the bedroom wing.

Yet this didn't feel right. Too easy. But he'd never credited Benjamin Sokolo with an overabundance of brains. The man ran on overconfidence and ego, not high I.Q.

Harkness signaled Damongo close, whispered an instruction. The tall Ghanaian relayed the order to the shorter man. The Ingrams were already cocked.

Harkness eased to the lighted central window, a broad expanse of glass that surely gave a magnificent view of the open sea below. Now, though, its translucent drapes were tightly drawn. He moved across the window to the adjacent entrance, raised his boot and slammed it into the wood just above the latch. This was to be a

215

shock assault. Smash in boldly, shoot everything that moved, bugger out just as fast.

The door flew open. Harkness rammed through first, the Ingram stuttering as momentum carried him well into the central great-room. Its 9-millimeter slugs tore jagged holes through a trio of nude paintings on the far wall, blew puffs of stuffing from the padded leather settee and its flanking chairs, sprayed shards of the two back windows into the night.

Behind him, the two Ghanaians had already split, Damongo veering left, Yendi to the right, each charging down the hallways off the great-room. As he crouched and deftly reloaded, Harkness heard the banging of doors in both halls, then the rivet gun stutters of their machine pistols clattered along the halls almost simultaneously. Harkness jerked back against the wall beside the ruined doorway and waited, nerves tight as wire springs. But they both trotted back in thirty seconds. No one anywhere. They had fired to let off tension or in frustration.

But why the lights?

There was nothing for it now but to get the hell out of here, return overland to Monrovia when the Evinrude ran dry, find out what went wrong. Plan the damned sortie all over again. Harkness cursed fitfully as he led his men back across the veranda and down the slope toward the beach. The bloody profit margin wasn't that wide.

They made it to the edge of the sand. Then the night flared into dazzling blue-white day. Floodlights, a whole battery of them concealed under the veranda's lip, caught them naked there, seventy yards from any conceivable shelter.

All of them dropped flat where they stood, facing the blinding floods. But the noise, then the slamming impact of steel-jacketed slugs came from the rocks that edged both sides of the beach.

Kalashnikovs, Harkness realized. You can tell by the sound. Then he died.

The hand-picked infantry detachment left the three corpses where they lay. When Sokolo and his small entourage returned at nine the following morning, vultures were becoming a problem. Colonel Botatu, in combat dress, triggered three shots from his service pistol into the air to clear them off when President Sokolo strode across the veranda and down the slope.

Sokolo turned and motioned to Kwame M'Tibi. "Mr. Bones, I want you to see what happens to enemies of the state."

M'Tibi had an idea what that meant. Only he, in addition to the president himself, knew that Sokolo's sudden departure from the vacation villa yesterday had been prompted not by Sokolo's vaunted ability to forecast the future. It had been spurred by a phone call from the Swiss Legation in the capital city. Now the president was warning M'Tibi to keep his mouth closed about that. The valet followed the dashiki-clad giant down the hill.

They gazed at the bodies. The sound of nearby surf blended with the buzz of a thousand flies to make M'Tibi feel oddly light-headed. Perhaps it was the sun, as well, beating down on his gray-wooled head.

Behind him, Colonel Botatu stood at a respectful distance with his eight green-uniformed infantrymen who had sprung last night's trap. They hadn't yet had breakfast and were hungry and bored with the long wait for the president to reappear to admire their work.

"Ingrams," Sokolo said. He bent with a grunt to pull the stubby gun from beneath the outflung arm of the white man. He studied the thing, aimed it out to sea, and pulled the trigger. A ripping burst brought new cries from the vultures circling overhead. He handed the Ingram to his valet to lug back up the hill for him.

"I will keep that for the presidential archives." To Colonel Botatu, he called, in a ribald effort to divert the grumbling soldiers and becoming grossly carried away with the euphoria of the moment, "A shame they brought no women soldiers with them. We could have had sport."

The buzzing and surf noises in M'Tibi's head suddenly swelled and blocked out all other sound. Across his vision flashed a chilling glimpse of his Kita, raped raw and bleeding by the men of Sokolo, dying of lolo poison and shame. And through a crimson film of fury, he pointed the boxy Ingram at the President of Nandia and jerked the trigger.

The eleven slugs remaining in the breech and magazine ripped Sokolo's middle out before Botatu was able to yank out his American-made .45 and blast Kwame M'Tibi three full paces forward, then flat down with all seven shots.

The echoes of gunfire dissolved in the surf's ceaseless wash. The flies settled again, now speckling five bodies. The vultures began to glide lower through the still air.

An infantry sergeant behind him muttered cynically, "Who is in charge now?"

"I am," said Colonel Botatu.

Dan hadn't slept much after the Maryland State Police interrogation; then the arm's-length questioning by the State Department's security people; next the unctuous but ultimately threatening CIA rep; then the three-piece-suited officious FBI agent-in-charge; plus the growing gantlet of media locusts who had somehow managed to gather wherever he and Corkie had been shunted.

Three days of that, plus trying to get the matter of the sunken Chevette resolved, more calls from and to Charlie, and two calls to Cousin Roy to help him clear his case record as promised—and which precipitated a dandy little jurisdictional dispute with the FBI over who had first grabs at J.B. Hammermill. All that, and Dan still couldn't sleep.

When dawn finally shadowed his barebones room on their final morning in Washington, Dan gave up trying. He stumbled on leaden feet to the bathroom, splashed his face with cold water, shaved, pulled on slacks and a shirt. Then he heard the connecting door open.

Same blue robe, but now he found it curiously reassuring. "You can't sleep either?"

"I'm still cold, Dan, so damned cold. Hot coffee, hot showers, extra threadbare blanket. I'm still so cold."

"We could have, if you'd wanted, gotten ourselves into a nice overheated downtown hotel," Dan reminded her. "Charlie might not have gone for it, but we could have talked State or the CIA or FBI into springing for rooms at the Mayflower or the Washington Hilton. They fell all over themselves to get at us."

"Kind of gave you a feeling of power, didn't it?"

"Not me, kid. I only wondered how to get a new raincoat out of *NewsLeak.*" He snorted. "Power? I did think we had something going with the story that could have . . ." He shrugged.

"Saved the guy? Saved the wrong guy?"

"Damned if I know how to look at it, Cork." He strapped on his watch. "We've got more than three hours before checkout time. Treat you to breakfast?"

"I'm cold, not hungry." She stood in the connecting doorway, eyes oddly luminous. "Don't you understand, Dan?"

He understood. He was cold, too, deep in his marrow, with the kind of frozen dread no mere scalding shower would ever thaw.

This time he did say it: "Oh, what the hell?" Some way to express what should have been something much more tender. But she wasn't a quibbler.

This, he realized, would be their first unguarded hello. But it had to be good-bye, too. And they both knew that. Maybe they would work together again, but they'd never do this together again, not this kind of totally vulnerable closeness.

But on this final morning in Largo, his stark room in the Barren Hilton took on a pleasant low-budget glow, as she slipped off the blue tent and slid under the blanket beside him. They were two survivors, the only two who could ever really know what they'd been through together. It was that kind of closeness.

There was a lot of her, all of it soft and unexpectedly sweet and, after a while, comfortably warm. And it took a wonderfully long time, because neither of them wanted to hurry. When she kissed him a last time, she whispered, "I'm not cold anymore, Daniel."

Then they packed, checked out with *NewsLeak*'s Amex card, and buckled themselves into their newly rented Toyota for the long drive home.